Voices in the Woods

Voices in the Woods

By DC Fidler

DCFidler Publishing
<2017>

Published by DCFidler Publishing
1117 University Avenue, #505
Morgantown, WV 26505
DCFidlerpublishing@gmail.com

Printed in the United States of America
by Lulu Press, Inc.

This play is entirely a work of fiction.
Any resemblance to actual persons, living or dead,
is entirely coincidental.

ISBN: 978-0-9989729-0-9
Library of Congress Control Number: 2017906601

Dedication

With deep appreciation and love for all my family and friends scattered throughout North Carolina and West Virginia. With deep appreciation and love for all of my Kodiak Alutiiq, Omani Moqbali, New Zealand, and Queensland Outback friends and adopted families. I thank all of you for decades of wondrous and loving porch-sitting, fire-gathering, and kitchen-sitting, story-telling sessions that propelled me to write this play. Should you recognize yourself in this play, I do not apologize to you, but instead, I say to you, "I adore you."

Acknowledgments

I have deep gratitude for friends, family members, and colleagues.

Catherine Telford for her unending energy and enthusiasm, encouraging me to turn a scene into a play, for critiquing the different versions of the script, and for bringing endearing life to the character of Precious Grace.

People, who generously spared time to generate ideas, help me edit early drafts, and participate in readings.

Kevin Marlow	Kate Zondlo
Dennis Marlow	Scott Snyder
Preston Mendenhall	Carol Paris
Joe Oliveri	Christopher Boyce
Doris Whitesides	Jim Brown
Beth Frampton	Bonnie Brown
Paul Frampton	David Wells
Bryan Caudill	Charlie Trumbull
Dan Moore	Liz Creech

People, who helped me with authenticity of names, locations, china patterns, speech styles, and much more.

Herb and Marion Ward-Roberts	Dr. Charles Neel
Irving and Becka Kuo	Cheryl Yeager
Bill and Dianne Trumbull	Nancy Wasson

And my "Don Kids," who inspired and encouraged me to initially write, *Voices in the Woods*.

Sam, Trey, Nicholas, Kevin, Dennis, and Stuart.

VOICES IN THE WOODS premiered at the MAC Theatre in Morgantown, West Virginia on Thursday, April 1, 1993.

Production Staff:

Director	Preston Mendenhall
Production Stage Manager	Brant Haas
Scenic Designer	Michael Halad
Costume Designer	Cheryl Yeager
Props	Rodney Boyer
Lighting Designer	Jed Haas

Cast:

PRECIOUS	Catherine Telford
BO	Brian Caudill
AUNT EULA	Nancy Wasson
UNCLE DWEZEL	Charles D. Neel
DWAYNE	Todd Farlow
BERTHA	Linda Zimmer
BRENT	Justin Nelms
TODD	Bob Riddle

VOICES IN THE WOODS opened at the Co-Op Pacific Resident Theatre Ensemble in Venice, California on October 5, 1995.

Production Staff:

Producers	Catherine Telford
	Channing Chase
Director	Martha Hackett
Production Stage Manager	Lara Wright
Scenic Designer	Bradley Kaye
	John Patrick
Costume Designer	Diane Puhalla
Props	Margy Stein
Lighting Designer	Kevin Monk

Cast:

PRECIOUS	Catherine Telford*
BO	Joe Olivieri*
AUNT EULA	Linda Lodge*
UNCLE DWEZEL	Frank Collison*
DWAYNE	Robert Lee Jacobs*
BERTHA	Suzanne Ford*
BRENT	Jarrett Berenstein
TODD	James Benton*

*Members of Associated Actors & Artists of America

Characters

PRECIOUS GRACE REAMY - a woman in her early 50s
BO RAY REAMY - a man in his early 50s
BERTHA SUE - a woman in her mid 40s
DWAYNE LEE REAMY - a man in his late 30s
EULA MAE FREMHACKER - a woman in her early 70s
DWEZEL BEECHER - a man in his late 70s
BRENT - a young teenage boy
TODD - a well-tanned, muscular man in his early 20s

Setting

Brantley Run, West Virginia. Aging country house kitchen and porch, summer 1995. The kitchen has a variety of chairs, tables, cabinets, a refrigerator, and a record player. The porch has chairs and benches, possibly a swing, an obvious site for socializing during hot weather. There are enough objects to hint the porch also serves as a storage area for almost anything. A screen door separates the kitchen from the porch. There is a bathroom door and a hallway door in the kitchen and stairs to the second-floor bedrooms.

Note

In contrast to formal scripts for use in rehearsals, this is a book of the script, containing more stage directions to aid readers to envision what can be happening upon the stage. Most actors prefer few or no directions, allowing them to discover and create the lives of their characters.

ACT ONE

PORCH AND KITCHEN
ON A WARM AUGUST AFTERNOON

Curtain rises on PRECIOUS sweeping the porch and humming a hymn. She enters the kitchen through a screen door and becomes occupied with kitchen work. BO enters from upstairs.

BO: Even on her deathbed, Mama is mean and she's devious.

PRECIOUS: Mama's jest a little upset 'cause she's dyin'.

BO: Mama's upset 'cause she's dying and I'm living. You know what she told me? She's up there acting like she's taking her last breath—

PRECIOUS: She's been doin' that fer thirty years.

BO: Taking her last breath, and she motions for me to come closer. I lean next to her pillow, and she whispers, "Bo Ray Reamy, your papa's not really your papa." Then passes out. That's an all-time record for Mama being mean.

PRECIOUS: Bo, don't make fun jest cuz I can't think how to best tell you this.

BO: Tell me what?

PRECIOUS: *(Carries plate of cookies from the stove to BO and hands him one.)* Papa's not yer papa.

BO: What?

1

PRECIOUS: Mama's not bein' mean. She probably jest thought you should know 'fore somebody fergits to tell ya. Would you like some milk with them cookies?

BO: How can Papa not be my papa?

PRECIOUS: Jest ain't.

BO: Mama and Papa were married for seven years before I was born. You and I are only eleven months apart.

PRECIOUS: Six.

BO: Six?

PRECIOUS: Six.

BO: Six what?

PRECIOUS: Six months apart.

BO: We can't be six months apart. We're brother and sister. Not even cows can be six months apart.

PRECIOUS: I reckon not, not if they have the same mama they can't.
(Serves a glass of milk to BO.)

BO: Wait a minute, wait a minute. You just said Papa's not my papa. Are you telling me Mama's not my mama?

PRECIOUS: Do you want more cookies to go with that milk?

BO: I didn't want the cookie that came before the milk. Precious, you better not be making up lies.

PRECIOUS: Jest cause a person has hallucinations, "a different perspective on life," don't mean they lie.

2

BO: How long have you known this?

PRECIOUS: That I have a different perspective?

BO: That Mama and Papa are not *my* mama and papa!

PRECIOUS: Since I wuz four. I'll join you fer cookies and milk. I give you the one with M&Ms. I'll eat the ones with peanut-butter morsels. I know you don't like smellin'em on yer breath.

BO: I don't like smelling peanut butter on *other* people's breath . . . Why do you think Mama's so mean?

PRECIOUS: *(Turns head away and covers mouth as eats.)* Lack'a stimulation, I guess. Last winter, when snow wuz all 'round the pump house, I found this tiny little dead bird. It's wing wuz broke, so I reckon it couldn't fly. Jest froze there in the snow. You know what Mama said?

BO: She broke its wing?

PRECIOUS: No. She said, "It must be awful bein' that little bird starvin' in the snow, watchin' our sty fulla hogs slop down more each minute than it ate in its entire life."

BO: Mama the philosopher.

PRECIOUS: Make fun'a Mama. We can't all leave West Virginia and go somewheres fancy like New York, or Detroit, or Greensboro, North Carolina. Write ads for ladies' magazines.

BO: Greensboro is not fancy.

PRECIOUS: I wouldn't know.

(Slides chair back from table, looks at ceiling, and screams.)
Not now! Later!
(Aruptly calms, moves back to table, and resumes eating.)

BO: Precious, honey? Did you take your medicine?

PRECIOUS: Why?

BO: Are you hallucinating?

PRECIOUS: No.

BO: Are you sure?

PRECIOUS: Yes.

BO: I think you are hearing things again.

PRECIOUS: Nope.

BO: I saw you hearing things.

PRECIOUS: You saw me hearin' things.

BO: I saw you hearing things.

PRECIOUS: You saw me hearin' things.

BO: I saw you hearing things.

PRECIOUS: You can't see people hearin' things, they's not visible. They said so.

BO: They said so? When?

PRECIOUS: Don't be tryin' to trick me. It makes you sound like Mama and I will not be condescended to.

BO: Sorry . . . So, if Mama and Papa are not my parents, who are?

PRECIOUS: Have you took one'a yer Valiums?

BO: Will I need one?

PRECIOUS: Mr. and Mrs. Franzini.

BO: Maybe I should take one of your pills.

PRECIOUS: Oh Bo, they really are stronger. You git this kind'a calmness that's hard to 'splain.

BO: The Franzinis.

PRECIOUS: Mr. Franzini helped Mama git pregnant.

BO: Helped?

PRECIOUS: Me and you is half brother and sister, Mr. Franzini bein' daddy to both'a us. Papa's not our daddy, Mr. Franzini is, but Mama's not yer mama, jest my mama. Mrs. Franzini's yer mother, or so she says. Bo, we have one slice'a strawberry-rhubarb pie left in the Frigidaire.

BO: When I woke this morning, I questioned whether I wanted to continue writing jingles for selling women's underwear. I had this pain telling me to change the way I look at myself.

PRECIOUS: See! Mama changed yer outlook fer you. And you thought she wuz bein' mean.

BO: She's not my mama!

PRECIOUS: Don't be silly. She raised you jest like you wuz her little boy. Jest 'cause she don't plan to mention you in her will don't mean—

BO: Not in her will!

PRECIOUS: She didn't tell you?

BO: She didn't tell me I'm not her son!

PRECIOUS: She don't like upsettin' you, Bo.

BO: I am president of the biggest women's-apparel ad agency in Greensboro, North Carolina. I have a dozen employees working for me. I'm important. I come home to Brantley Run and one conversation over M&M cookies with my sister and my entire existence is obliterated!

PRECIOUS: Oh, Bo, I see why Mama never used to tell you nothin'. You git so excited. Maybe she wuz right to never tell you 'bout the sex-change operation.

BO: The what?

PRECIOUS: Never mind.
(Carries cookie plate to the sink.)

BO: The sex-change operation?

(PRECIOUS shakes her head and answers with unintelligible mumbles with her mouth full of cookie.)

BO: Whose sex-change operation?

PRECIOUS: Nothin' that won't hurt you not to know about.

BO: Precious, look at me. Whose sex-change operation?

PRECIOUS: Papa's.

BO: Papa's?

PRECIOUS: Papa's.

BO: Our papa's or . . . our daddy's?

PRECIOUS: Not our Mr. Franzini daddy but our Mr. Reamy papa.

BO: Both Mama and Papa are women?

PRECIOUS: Silly. Not since the operation.

BO: I think I will have that piece of strawberry-rhubarb pie.

PRECIOUS: Watchin' Mama die does work up yer appetite. Aunt Eula will be here at quarter'a four.
(Serves piece of pie to Bo.)

BO: Did she call?

PRECIOUS: It's Wednesday. Eula comes by at quarter'a four, unless it's snowin', then she comes at two-thirty.

BO: Does Thursday have a big event?

PRECIOUS: Uncle Dwezel drives his pickup over with a pound'a birdfeed.

BO: And Friday?

PRECIOUS: Uncle Norville brings the latest Polaroids of Charmain's children in the tub.

BO: Who scheduled all of this?

PRECIOUS: Papa. Jest 'fore he died.
(Carries calendar to BO.)
Tuesdays is daisy shoppin' days, only we didn't daisy shop yesterday on account'a Mama's dyin'. Wednesdays is rainbow days. Me and Mama wake up and draw a rainbow. And a tiny little pot'a gold, right here at the bottom. Then I put three nickels and a dime in my little pot behin' the ironin'-room radiator. Mama adds more. My pot'a gold. Thursdays is lightnin' days and Fri—

BO: What do you do on lightning days?

PRECIOUS: In spring and summer, water the flowers. Ten after nine 'til twenty-two after nine. In winter—

BO: Not a second more or less.

PRECIOUS: Ten after nine 'til twenty-two after nine!

BO: Okay, okay. Ten after nine.

PRECIOUS: *(Holds broom and reads the writing on the handle.)* "Each person has his job and must do his job superbly." Papa carved that on the broom handle. Ten after nine 'til twenty-two after nine. Lightnin' days.

BO: Lightning days.

PRECIOUS: *(Grabs pie plate as BO starts to take a bite and carries it to sink.)* Well, Eula should be here in a hour. Whatever you do, don't mention nothin' about her little—
(Whispers.)
problem.

BO: What little—
(Whispers.)
problem?

8

PRECIOUS: Her propensity toward klept whatever.

BO: What is klept whatever?

PRECIOUS: (Whispers.) Borrowin' things.

BO: Kleptomania?

PRECIOUS: Shhh, Bo.

BO: Aunt Eula steals things?

PRECIOUS: Somebody might could hear you.

BO: Who? The only thing that pulls Mama from her coma is championship wrestling. What kinds of things does Eula steal?

PRECIOUS: Oh, silver, china, fried chicken.

BO: Mercy. How long has she been doing this?

PRECIOUS: Best we can speculate, twenty-five year.

BO: Twenty-five—No one has said anything?

PRECIOUS: Now, don't go gittin' no wrong idea. It's little things no one's gonna miss. Except that time with Mr. Gilmore's cash register. You know how Eula's worked down at Motel Eleven twenty-five year? Mama learnt Eula took a little somethin' every day. Well, three little somethin's every day. A roll of toilet paper, a bar'a soap, and a washcloth.

BO: For twenty-five years?

PRECIOUS: Neatly stacked up in her guest bedroom. So full me and Mama can't pry open the door.

BO: How did this get started?

PRECIOUS: We noticed it about the time Eula got a giant freezer fer her back porch. Wound a chain 'round it with a over-sized padlock.

BO: When did she buy all of that?

PRECIOUS: I don't know she 'xactly bought them. September third, 1967.

BO: How on earth can you remember dates?

PRECIOUS: September third, 1967. The day after Uncle Will disappeared.

BO: Aunt Eula bought a giant freezer and padlocked it the day after Uncle Will disappeared?

PRECIOUS: Uh huh.

BO: The husband she swore she'd get rid of?

PRECIOUS: Me and Mama tried to peer into that freezer when Eula got her gall bladder took out, but she wore the key tied 'round her neck. Made Doc Pendergas *swear* not to remove it.

BO: When he had her under, you could have busted into that freezer.

PRECIOUS: Mama, the Sheriff, Butch Holler all tried. Eula wrapped it in a sawmill chain. Can't cut it, not even with the jaws'a life.

BO: Sweet Aunt Eula kleptomanisizes human bodies.

PRECIOUS: Bo Ray Reamy! That's the most despicable trash I ever heard tell anybody accuse our family of.

10

What if Mama heard you accusin' her darlin' sister of homicidal intentions?
(Sets a small basket of cookies on table.)

BO: Mama can't hear because Mama refuses to hear.

PRECIOUS: Bo, the big city life has transformed you into a not very nice person with an uncarin' and suspicious nature.

BO: I'm not the one stealing toilet paper and soap, or lying in a coma, miraculously arising at the smell of chicken-fried steak.

PRECIOUS: Bo, you need to come home more often and reclaim yerself.

BO: Could be, Precious.
(Starts to eat cookie.)

PRECIOUS: *(Yells as grabs cookie.)* Don't eat them! Them's fer Eula.

BO: You try to bust me with gallons of milk and cookies one minute and then the next—
(Lifts another cookie from basket and examines it.)
Your cookies have blue M&Ms.

PRECIOUS: Put that cookie back in the basket.

BO: I remember red M&Ms disappeared for about a decade. Came back one Christmas unannounced, but I've never seen . . . Precious! These aren't blue M&Ms! These are your pills!

PRECIOUS: *Bo Ray! Put them cookies in the basket!*

BO: You're poisoning people!

PRECIOUS: I ain't poisonin' nobody. I take them blue pills three times a day.

BO: Was there dope in the cookie you fed me?

PRECIOUS: It's not dope. It's Stelazine.

BO: What'll that do? Make my hair fall out? Reverse puberty?

PRECIOUS: Them wuz sugar-coated chocolates made by M&Ms.

BO: Positively? I'm not hallucinating that I'm trapped here in hell?

PRECIOUS: Bo Ray! Git a grip!

EULA: *(Yells from porch.)* Yoo hoo!
(Barges in, carrying a large purse and a large shopping bag.)
Anybody home?

PRECIOUS: Aunt Eula! Yer early.

EULA: Up and 'bout runnin' early errands. Shirley's hearin' aid battery went dead. Never makes it past the fifth of the month, but no, Shirley's gotta have his battery go dead and thump it three hours 'fore he'll replace it. Well, Bo Ray Reamy. Welcome home, baby.

BO: Aunt Eula.

EULA: I see that Californie sister of your'n ain't made it back to ole West Virginie yet.

BO: No ma'am, not yet.

EULA: Well Precious, is that a fresh batch of M&M cookies?

PRECIOUS: Sure is.

BO: No! Aunt Eula. Uh, the eggs were kind of rotten when I helped Precious mix the batter.

EULA: Hush, Bo Ray. I don't know nothin' better in Brantley Run to settle my nerves than one'a Precious' M&M cookies.

PRECIOUS: *(Holds up basket of cookies.)* Here ya go.

EULA: Why thank you, Precious darlin'.
(Tastes cookie and drops several into her purse.)
Hope you don't mind if I gather a few fer the road. Three of these a day and I feel like a new woman. Did I tell you about the chrysanthemum women's circle lecture I give over at the church parsonage?

PRECIOUS: I don't believe you have this week.

EULA: Well, I had jest went there when all of a sudden—

BO: Gone.

EULA: Pardon me, Bo?

BO: Gone. You had gone there, ma'am, Aunt Eula.

PRECIOUS: Bo suggests you said, "went," when you meant, "gone."

EULA: I know what Bo Ray suggests, Precious darlin'. But I distinctly had *went* there. I had *went* there, Bo. If I wuz to go to Boston, or New York, or wuz to attend a meetin' at yer ole alma mata, I would say *gone* instead of *went*. Jest like in 1958, I spoke French in Paris. Jest

13

like in 1963, Will spoke in tongues when we visited Raymond Fester's Holy Roller Church. Jest like last week I spoke baby-talk to my Sunday School three-year-olds. But when I talk to Precious, or even to you, when you happen to be treadin' on this fine West Virginia soil, then I speak in the language of Brantley Run. I had *went* to the parsonage, not *gone*. *Gone* is the past participle in yer ad agency. *Went* is the past participle in Brantley Run. Everybody knows that. Everybody has *knowed* that fer generations. The French Quebec Rebels made their stance fer French to be *spoke* in Montreal, and Eula Mae Fremhacker is makin' her stance fer *went* in Brantley Run! Now, where wuz I, Precious?

PRECIOUS: You were about to had *went* to the parsonage to—

EULA: Yes, yes, yes! Beautiful chrysanthemums! Beautiful! We wuz settin' there mindin' our own business, when that brother'a your'n come crashin' that rebuilt convertible pickup into the ladies-circle-number-four flowerbed. Needless to say, Beula Brantley superseded her pacemaker. Fell out on the parsonage floor. Drooled all over the Oriental rug circle number three donated with their winnin's from the state-fair Spam bakeoff.

PRECIOUS: Was Dwayne Lee hurt?

EULA: Hurt? Darlin', he wuz only goin' five mile a hour. He missed the curve 'cause he wuz standin' in his convertible pickup, drivin' with his toes.

PRECIOUS: With his toes?

EULA: Paradin' past his comrades at Buddy's Amoco. Moonin' his be-hind at'em.

PRECIOUS: Oh, my.

EULA: Do you mind if I sponge off in yer sink? I feel rather flushed.

PRECIOUS: Go right ahead, Eula. I can't picture Dwayne Lee showin' his hiney . . .

EULA: *(Picks up dishcloth and wipes her underarms.)* Spongin' over the sink is the most ecological way to bath all possible. I don't have no use fer no bathtub inside my house.

PRECIOUS: You use yer bathtub.

EULA: Fer oranges. That ceramic monstrosity keeps'em cool.

BO: You have a bathtub full of oranges?

EULA: In the spring, I store my 'maters in it. I told Will, installin' a bathtub wuz a waste.

BO: Unlike other modern conveniences. Say . . . a giant freezer?

(PRECIOUS dramatically frowns at BO.)

EULA: Would you two persons excuse me a tiny moment? I drank three glasses'a parsonage water and ain't been able to take care'a nature.
(Walks toward bathroom.)

PRECIOUS: Not that bathroom, Aunt Eula! That's where Grandpa Beecher died!

EULA: My golly, Precious Reamy!
(Grabs a salt shaker, pours salt into her hand, throws salt over shoulder, and rapidly spins around three times.)

Why don't you board that bathroom up before somebody sits on that thing and gits po·ssessed?

PRECIOUS: Mama likes to keep flowers and candles 'round the base and kneel and remember Grandpa.

EULA: Liked to give me a heart attack. I swan de goodness. *(Exits upstairs, carrying shopping bag.)*

BO: Dwayne was right. We should have adopted children. Not chance passing on family genetics.

PRECIOUS: But you and Dwayne Lee don't have the same genetics. I 'splained you how—

BO: Never mind!

(DWEZEL enters from porch without knocking.)

PRECIOUS: Uncle Dwezel. What a surprise!

BO: Hello, Uncle Dwezel.
(Stands and extends hand to shake with Dwezel.)
I haven't seen you in, I don't know when.

DWEZEL: *(Oblivious, walks straight to cookie basket.)*
You don't say. Goodness. Them look mighty good.

BO: No!

PRECIOUS: Jest a moment, Uncle Dwezel.
(Gets a small jar of cookies from shelf.)
These is yer cookies.

BO: Can I have one, too, Precious?

PRECIOUS: Do you have thyroid problems?

BO: You can't be doing this!

16

DWEZEL: Doin' what?

BO: Baking cookies. I mean, giving, I mean, Uncle Dwezel, I hate to say this, but those cookies Precious feeds you, have powerful medications in them.

DWEZEL: A course they do. Fer my high-boy.
(Points to his thyroid.)
Never could swallow them darn blasted pills. This way, I never know which bite's gonna be sweet and which bite's gonna taste like the dickens.

PRECIOUS: Now Bo, don't you feel silly?

DWEZEL: *(Bites cookie and makes a sour face.)* Dad blast it! I hate when it's the first bite! Precious Grace, can't you bake them high-boy pills in the middle?
(Bites cookie and smiles.)
That's better . . . Precious darlin'? With yer ma dyin' and all, I thought it best to pull my camper into yer lane. Sleep close by.

PRECIOUS: Oh, Uncle Dwezel, that's so sweet. You sure you don't want to sleep in Dwayne Lee's old room?

DWEZEL: Camper'll do, thank ya kindly.

BO: Uncle Dwezel, why do you need to camp in our driveway? Don't you live next door?

PRECIOUS: Bo Ray Reamy! If Uncle Dwezel wants to be in our lane while Mama's dyin', then that's a sweet gesture that shall remain unchallenged.

EULA: *(Re-enters with streams of toilet paper dangling from her shopping bag.)* Hello, Dwezel. Is that yer camper in the lane?
(Slides the cookie basket into her purse.)

17

BO: He's spending the night in our driveway, since he can't park in our kitchen.

EULA: I hadn't thought about sleepin' in my camper. Bo Ray, could you drive my camper over here and park it behind Dwezel's?

BO: I didn't know you had a camper.

EULA: Dwezel give me his '83 Winnebago. Bought himself a '72 Winnebago. Said the '83 model reminded him too much of Glenda Jo—God rest her soul. That camper wuz the last time the two of them slept together. Ain't that right, Dwezel?

DWEZEL: No, that was the 1957 Air Streamer. The 1957—

EULA: I said *slept*, not . . . whatever.

DWEZEL: Oh, slept. Yep. '83 Winnebago.

BO: I'm going upstairs for a moment, if you three don't mind.
(Exits upstairs.)

EULA: Precious Grace, I hope you don't divulge no family secrets in front'a Bo Ray.

PRECIOUS: I do believe he is a member of this family.

EULA: Yer mama never saw fit to share nothin' with the boy.

PRECIOUS: That's 'cause Bo has a peculiar propensity to over-react.

EULA: Well, I'd frown upon him gittin' snoopy.

PRECIOUS: Aunt Eula, Bo can't see no sun in the sky if you don't point his nose at it.

BO: *(Partially re-enters.)* Pardon me, Precious. All toilet paper seems to have disappeared off the roller. In fact, the roller seems to be missing.

PRECIOUS: *(Motions BO to shhh.)* Well, Bo, why don't you check the bathroom cupboard?

BO: Amazingly, the cupboard is absent of all toilet paper. As well as soap and tarter-gel toothpaste. I believe a washcloth or two may be missing.

EULA: *(Abruptly stands.)* Well, I best be goin'. I got lot'a folk to visit up and down the holler.

BO: Need a larger shopping bag, Aunt Eula? Something with the Motel-Eleven logo on it?

EULA: I got plenty in my Oldsmobile, Bo Ray, but thank ya kindly. Bye, Precious, honey.
(Gives PRECIOUS a kiss and nods to DWEZEL)
Bye, Bo. Hope you find yer misplaced toiletries.
(Exits outside.)

PRECIOUS: Oh, I hope she's not offended by yer accusations. Somebody should say somethin' nice to her.
(Runs to the porch door and yells.)
I like yer new hair color, Eula! It looks much more natural than that last color!

DWEZEL: *(Speaks as he rushes outside.)* I better make sure she don't sneak into my Winnebago and take all my denture paste agin.

BO: She robbed all our toilet paper!

PRECIOUS: The store closed fer inventory. You'll jest have to improvise.

BO: I'll get some from Dwezel.

PRECIOUS: Eula kleptomanified him yesterday.

BO: We don't even have *Kleenex* in this house! Mama keeps it all stuffed down her bosom.

(PRECIOUS throws a catalogue to BO.)

BO: What's this? Oh, no! No, no, no. That's like all the bad jokes anyone ever made about West Virginia. I could never look people straight in the eye.

PRECIOUS: Suit yerself.

BO: *(Pauses and then grabs catalogue.)* If you ever tell a single soul—

PRECIOUS: Bo, yer what Oprah calls, "image conscious."

BO: What the . . . This is my women's underwear catalogue! These are my models: Michelle, Jennifer, Rona.

(BO exits as PRECIOUS laughs and resumes cleaning. DWAYNE enters without speaking, walks to the refrigerator, gets milk, gets a plate of cookies, sits, and carefully examines several cookies inches from his face before he eats one.)

PRECIOUS: I understand you ought to cover certain parts'a that convertible pickup'a your'n.

(DWAYNE frowns and turns away.)

PRECIOUS: *(Retrieves a jar from cabinet.)* You caused the parsonage Oriental rug to git drooled on.

DWAYNE: Mind yer own beeswax.

PRECIOUS: Here, when you git a chance, baby brother, run this jar over to the Jello twins.

DWAYNE: What's in it?

PRECIOUS: Sorghum.

DWAYNE: What do four-year-old boys need with sorghum?

PRECIOUS: *(Hispanic pronunciation of names.)* Orangejello and Lemonjello won't eat roast beef that ain't drowned in Mama's sorghum.
(Places jar on table.)

BO: *(Enters.)* I can't. I'd be constipated a week from the backward repulsion I felt . . . Oh, hello, Dwayne.

(DWAYNE continues eating.)

BO: We were just talking about you, or Aunt Eula was. Said a butt-load of people got to view you in your self-styled convertible pickup.

DWAYNE: I gotta go.
(Hurriedly exits.)

BO: Nice brotherly exchange.

PRECIOUS: Dwayne Lee gits in them moods. Mama says, "No pride, no small talk."

BO: I call it, "rudeness."

PRECIOUS: You're still mad 'cause'a that barn door.

21

BO: How would you feel if someone told you to jump up and down on a barn door lying in a field, said it'd make a musical sound? And then a ton of cow shit squirts up all over your legs.

(PRECIOUS laughs as returns jar to cabinet.)

BO: Laugh like everybody else. How come Dwayne Lee has more photos in Mama's room than I have?

PRECIOUS: He's the baby! Besides, he's got 'xactly the same number.

BO: His are single photos. Mine are group photos. Mama doesn't have one photo of me by myself.

PRECIOUS: Why is that? Oh! That's right. Mama told me. Bo, will you help me git the double boiler out?

BO: Told you what?

BERTHA: *(Enters, carrying purse and designer shopping bag, and screams with joy.)* Oh! Precious! Bo! *(Enthusiastically hugs them, continuing to scream.)*

PRECIOUS: Bertha Sue!

BERTHA: My big brother and sister! Look at you! Oh, my goodness. You two look . . . country.

PRECIOUS: You look like a movie star.

BERTHA: When you live in California, you can't help but look star-like. It's in the ambiance.

BRENT: *(Enters, carrying a sports bag.)* Like this is Grandma's house? No sidewalks. Like where's a dude skateboard, man?

BERTHA: Brent, this is your Aunt Precious Grace Reamy and Uncle Bo Ray Reamy.

(PRECIOUS extends her hand but BRENT puts his hands behind his back.)

BRENT: Uh . . . Hi.

PRECIOUS: Look at you. Yer so big! Come gimme a hug.

BRENT: Like let's be real.

PRECIOUS: Yer so handsome I could squeeze ya to death.

BRENT: Mom!

BERTHA: Go on!

(BRENT whispers into BERTHA'S ear.)

BERTHA: *(Whispers.)* It's not contagious.

PRECIOUS: Oh, that's okay, Bertha Sue. Boys don't like huggin'. Let me git you some chocolate milk.

BRENT: Like I don't think so.

BERTHA: Young man, I'm not warning you again.

BRENT: I see your neighbors have refrigerators and couches on their porches. Bet that increases property values. Nice community bylaws!

BERTHA: Brent! Well, the old home place looks . . . like the old home place.

(TODD enters carrying suitcases and sets them on the floor.)

23

BERTHA: Oh, Bo, Precious, I want you to meet Todd. Todd, this is my sister Precious and my brother Bo.

PRECIOUS: Oh, Todd! Yer Bertha's new husband!

BERTHA: Uh . . . That was a different Todd. We went across the Nevada line and had our marriage annulled. This is Todd . . . my friend.

PRECIOUS: You already divorced yer third husband?

BERTHA: Fourth. California fast track. Todd, this Todd, and I are not marrying. We're just living together. Planning to have a couple of kids. If I can. We sure are trying!

PRECIOUS: Without marryin', Bertha Sue?

BERTHA: California.

PRECIOUS: Well, I never.

BERTHA: Bo, which room will we be using?

BO: Oh, just move from room to room as the urge strikes you.

BERTHA: Cute. Brent, why don't you carry our things upstairs? You and Todd can look around.

BRENT: Oh, goody. And like what do you suggest after those two intriguing minutes?

BERTHA: Brent!

BRENT: Come on, Todd. Fetch.

(TODD picks up suitcases and sports bag, and exits upstairs.)

BRENT: At least he's better than the last Todd. He wrote "cosmic poetry" and painted happy faces on soybeans. *(Exits upstairs.)*

BERTHA: God, he's a handsome surfer, isn't he?

BO: Can follow directions, too.

BERTHA: Bo, don't make it a mistake I flew all the way from California, dragging Brent from his skateboard exhibition.
(Pause.)
How's . . .

BO: Not good. This time, the doctor says she's not good.

BERTHA: Could I have something to drink?

PRECIOUS: Lipton Tea, chocolate milk, R.C. Cola, Matt's Roadside Stand Apple Juice—

BERTHA: Anything with alcohol?

PRECIOUS: Uh . . . not unless there's some'a Papa's MD 20/20 still under—

BERTHA: Any seltzer?

PRECIOUS: Seltzer?

BO: No, Bertha. And no sprouts or Perrier.

BERTHA: God, it's great to be back, isn't it?

BO: It is good.

BERTHA: Bo, the romantic, seeing beauty in these flower-covered hills. Oblivious to rusted coal machinery poking through.

BO: California fits you well, Bertha. I thought you would have changed your name. Phoebee, Zsa Zsa.

PRECIOUS: We got well water. It's low in calories and has minerals.

BERTHA: That's sweet, Precious.
(Stares out window as PRECIOUS gets water.)
There's still a strand of rope hanging from the sugar maple. Right where Uncle Shirley and Papa tied it. I loved that old swing more than anything I ever owned or touched. Remember when Charlie Higgins smeared dog hormones on the rope and we couldn't understand why Bear Dog kept trying to hump the swing and hump us every time we touched that swing? Papa was so mad. I wonder what ever happened to Charlie Higgins.

PRECIOUS: Prison.

BERTHA: Oh . . . So, how long does mother have?

BO: Mother? Mama has . . . I don't know, Bertha. It's not like the movies. I can't answer, "minutes" or "hours." No music swells when the end is near.

BRENT: *(Runs down stairs.)* Excellence! There's an entire video arcade next to the old sleeping dame. Requires quarters. Can you believe that? So cool!
(Runs up the stairs.)

BERTHA: That's your Grandmother Reamy!

(Sound of video game noises and explosions.)

PRECIOUS: Oh! Mama's outta her coma. I best make sure she's got plenty'a quarters. She has conniptions if she don't.
(Exits up steps.)

(BERTHA and BO move outside to porch.)

BERTHA: Why in hell didn't Sumter and the kids come with you?

BO: Sumter still thinks she's an old-school Georgia deb. Interested in happy things. How things smell. How nice things look. Junior League. Chantilly China. Not "tacky, trashy" Brantley Run, watching an old woman dying.

BERTHA: Mama always said Sumter's bosoms and head went well together, both overly large and both lacking in purpose.

BO: She does have an allergy to thinking. To think, you have to tolerate unhappiness. For Sumter, everything has to be clean, ordered. After we make love, and love can be chaotic—

BERTHA: Oh god, can't it!

BO: She insists we change the linens, straighten up the bed in case the boys walk in the next morning. I need a partner, a companion. Sumter's stuck reliving episodes of *Donna Reed*, hair perfectly teased, the children saying, "Oh, golly gee."

BERTHA: What's she going to do when the boys start dealing crack?

BO: Hutton got a girl pregnant. Jason got a ticket for driving under the influence. Sumter said, "We don't talk about things like that. Now, who wants chocolate-layer cake?"

BERTHA: As Brent would say, "Gag me with a spoon, dude."

BO: Well, she was the type of girl Mama pushed me to date.

BERTHA: She was not! Mama thought Sumter was the stupidest person she ever met.

BRENT: *(Rushes down the stairs, grabs his mother's purse, shakes out quarters, and yells out the screen-door.)* That old chick's bitchin' at Saturn Predators. Dusted my ass! Won't share her quarters though. Thanks, Mom!
(Rushes back upstairs.)

BERTHA: Do you spank your kids?

BO: Goodness no. I shame them to death.

BERTHA: Mama and Papa didn't prepare me to raise a California child. My therapist said, "Use rewards and praise." For rewards, Brent chose lying on a raft in our condo pool while having sex with two girls.

PRECIOUS: *(Enters from upstairs and walks to porch door.)* Bo, I'm gonna put Frey Varley's Dresden-pattern quilt on yer bed instead of that ole army blanket. Where'd'ya find that ole blanket anyhow?

BO: When Frostwillow was a colt, I warmed him with that blanket.

PRECIOUS: Terrible shame Frostwillow died.

BO: He would have made a fine horse.

PRECIOUS: You'd probably rather keep it. I'll—

BO: No, no, it was just the first thing I could find.

PRECIOUS: The house feels like we wuz kids agin. Papa would love us talkin' and laughin', spinnin' stories. *(Exits upstairs.)*

BERTHA: What's going to happen to Precious?

BO: She can have the house. You and I sure as heck don't need it, don't want it.

BERTHA: She can't manage this house.

BO: She stands up to Mama. Cleans. Gardens. Plans all the meals.

BERTHA: Mama deplores Precious' cooking, just tolerates it to keep her busy. Mama wanted to move away a long time ago. Share a place with Aunt Gypsy Branch in South Carolina.

BO: Precious would have followed her.

BERTHA: Once, Mama and Papa took Precious to Baltimore, the sea aquarium. Precious absolutely lost her wits. They had to hospitalize her.

BO: I never heard about that.

BERTHA: Mama didn't want to disturb your career. Medication didn't help. Precious became stiff as a board. You could have used her for a hat rack. They brought her home. Suddenly, little miss homemaker. Busy as a bee.

BO: At least she'll be here, home.

BERTHA: Home's leaving these walls. Mama always made sure to keep Precious in her sight, except when she took Papa down to Charleston for chemotherapy. When they came home, Precious had the house immaculate. Dusted, washed. Precious, on the other hand, hadn't showered, hadn't eaten. Sitting here on the porch, humming hymns.

BO: We can hire someone to come here and live with her.

BERTHA: Mama tried a private nurse. Precious hid in her closet.

BO: This is sad.

BERTHA: You must have had blinders on, big brother.

BO: I was building a life. For me, for Sumter, for the boys. At least I didn't fly off to California.

BERTHA: I call Mama and Precious every week. I don't disappear from their hearts for years at a time.

BO: This house is a cemetery. When I'm here, I feel like I'm in a little pine coffin, suffocating. Story after story about family peculiarities, how I'm destined to inherit family peculiarities, and my children, and my children's children.

BERTHA: So, you drop in here, cry a few tears when Mama dies, then escape for good. Do you know how broken-hearted Papa was when you stayed away so long?

BO: I don't want to hear this.
(Returns to kitchen.)

BERTHA: *(Follows BO.)* He used to brush off home plate on that little ball field he built, praying you might bring his grandsons home to play a game.

BO: I couldn't! I can't even talk to this family every week. My sanity soars right out there with Precious'.

BERTHA: And Mama's hoping you'll be the one to watch after her.

BO: Me? I have my own family, my own business!

BERTHA: Maybe Sumter's not the only one who wants everything happy.
(Holds up a catalogue.)
Dress up life with fancy colorful photography. Photograph women in underwear, smiling . . . No dirt.
(Slings catalogue at BO and exits into hallway.)

BO: At least I don't change the characters in my life every couple of years! Or is it every couple of months now?

PRECIOUS: *(Enters from upstairs.)* What's all the mess? Mama can hardly hear her Ninja Dragon game.

BO: Nothing, little sister. Bertha gets to me sometimes.

PRECIOUS: Gonna have children and not git married. Goodness, Bo. What's Bertha Sue comin' to?

BO: A different world, Precious, a different . . . Well, I never finished unpacking.
(Climbs a few steps.)

PRECIOUS: Oh, Bo?
(Points to places at the table as if people are sitting there.)

Ain't it grand havin' Bertha Sue, and Dwayne Lee, and you, and Uncle Dwezel, and Aunt Eula, and everybody home agin? Ain't this jest the grandest?

BO: Yeah, Precious Grace, it's awful grand.

(They freeze in place for a moment and then the lights go down to black.)

ACT TWO

MORNING IN THE KITCHEN

Prior to the lights rising, there is the sound of a toilet flushing. Lights rise on BO standing at the stove, cooking a large breakfast.

BRENT: *(Enters from bathroom door, tucking in his shirt and zipping his pants.)* Coolness, man. First time I've like had a colossal experience of pinching a loaf on a throne, little candles burning around my feet.

BO: Don't let Precious Grace know you inaugurated the mausoleum. Want some breakfast? I'm fixing.

BRENT: *Fixing?*

BO: *Making* breakfast. In California, you *make* it. In West Virginia, we *fix* it.

BRENT: What are you . . . *fixing*, dude?

BO: A little eggs, country ham, red-eye gravy, grits and butter, toast, apple butter, biscuits, sausage-milk gravy, coffee, orange juice. Things you fix.

BRENT: Just *make* me oat bran with two-percent.

BO: Making's easier than fixing. Where did you go last night?

BRENT: Fishing. Unk Dwayne reeled me in a fourteen incher.

BO: In a lightning storm?

BRENT: Totally heroic. The man's a marvel in adversity.

BO: One view of Dwayne Lee, I suppose.

BRENT: No wonder the 1978-Brantley-Run Prom Queen married the dude.

BO: Prom Queen. Hmm. What'cha doing up so early?

BRENT: Habit, dude.

BO: Habit dude?

BRENT: Skateboarding, dude.

BO: Ah, skateboarding. A dude with a goal.

BRENT: What's your goal?

BO: Gripping onto the vestiges of my sanity.

BRENT: Dude? Have you like been doing drugs?

BO: More intense. Conversing with the family.

>*(DWEZEL and DWAYNE enter from porch and sit at kitchen table.)*

BO: Morning Uncle Dwezel, Dwayne.

>*(They don't acknowledge. DWEZEL sits as DWAYNE and BRENT silently perform a secret ritual of a lengthy handshake and dance.)*

BO: Would you like me to make you some breakfast?

DWAYNE: *(Sits.)* Make me some breakfast?

BRENT: He means, "fix."

DWAYNE: Fix. Oh, no thank you.

DWEZEL: Speakin'a county municipal landfills, the county is all in an uproar over this garbage thing. The Feds wants us to haul in red clay to fill the bottom'a the landfill, then gravel, then buy special plastic liners to allow percolation. That'd cost a million dollar per acre. I know good and well, and I told that Fed lady so, big cities don't conform to that. Children and education is our future, but so's garbage!

DWAYNE: Yes, *but,* I played basketball in the church league yesterday with Snowy Foster and Bunky and Trout Fitch. We lost by *twen-ty-se-ven* points. Jest 'cause the Calvary Baptists let Rhonda Jo Singletary play center. A *girl!* Heck, she could go pro if she wanted. Not fair!

DWEZEL: Yep, that's the truth, Dwayne Lee, *but,* where does Cleveland dump all her garbage? She don't spend no million dollar per acre. She leave it pile up on streets long enough rain percolates it down the gutters, right into Lake Erie.

DWAYNE: Yer on top'a it, *but,* if they's gonna bring in pro players, even if they's girls, and I don't care if they's girls, long as they don't mix'em up in junior high, then they shouldn't use Methodists and call'em Baptists, jest so they can play.

DWEZEL: I know what you mean, Dwayne Lee.

DWAYNE: I'm with you, Uncle Dwezel.

BRENT: Dude, holding onto the vestiges of your sanity is beyond possibility.
(Pats BO on back and grabs fishing rod and tackle box. To DWAYNE.)
Wish me luck, Unk.

DWAYNE: Wool socks?

(BRENT shows his socks, gives the thumbs up sign, and walks toward door.)

DWAYNE: Whoa, son. *Never, never* crease yer hat on the edges. Crease the middle.
(Alters BRENT'S hat.)
Yer from Brantley Run, not Grafton.

(DWYANE and BRENT again perform the secret handshake and dance, and additionally end with pretending to smoke joints. BRENT exits and sits on porch.)

DWAYNE: *(Nods to BO.)* Fishin'.
(Sits.)

DWEZEL: So, Bo, what'chu doin' these days?

BO: Well, I'm still CEO of my ad agency in North Carolina.

DWAYNE: Photographs women in underwear.

DWEZEL: Is that a fact?

BO: Well, for ads, yes.

DWEZEL: Tell me everythin' about it.

BO: Well, about eleven years ago—

DWEZEL: I knowed a man once, lived in Omaha, where is that Dwayne?

DWAYNE: Nebraska.

DWEZEL: Omaha, Nebraska. Yep. I knowed a man from Omaha, Nebraska. He knowed more about the Civil War than anybody I ever knowed. Sure did. Yep. He sure did.

(BO moves chair away from table, reads newspaper, and drinks coffee.)

DWAYNE: Yeah, but every time I take Michelle and Dwayne Junior bowlin', and don't invite their mom, she accuses me'a tryin' to turn our kids agin her. What do you think, Bo?

BO: Well, Dwayne, there are times I try not to think. Not to listen. Not to talk. Not try to make sense of things.

PRECIOUS: *(Enters from upstairs.)* Good morning, Uncle Dwezel, Dwayne.

BO: Good morning, Precious.

PRECIOUS: Anybody want me to fix some breakfast?

DWEZEL: Bless you, Precious child. Me and Dwayne Lee wuz jest settin' here starvin'.

DWAYNE: Can't do a day's work without breakfast stuck to yer ribs.

PRECIOUS: Bo? You off in yer own little world?

BO: Nope. No matter how hard I try. Nope.

PRECIOUS: Wha'da we got here? My goodness! Eggs, country ham, red-eye gravy, grits and butter, toast, apple butter, biscuits, sausage-milk gravy, coffee, orange juice. What'da ya'll want?

DWEZEL: You got oat bran with two-percent?

PRECIOUS: Sure do.

DWAYNE: Me, too.

PRECIOUS: Me, too.

BO: Wait a minute! Doesn't anyone eat a big breakfast anymore?

DWEZEL: Doc said not to. Gotta git my cholesterol numbers down twenty.

DWAYNE: I eat a big breakfast when out-a-state folk come visit.

DWEZEL: Out-a-state folk complain about how unhealthy big breakfasts is, but everything you stuff under their face? They gobble it down!

PRECIOUS: *(Serves cereal.)* Here ya go.

DWEZEL: Thank you, child. How's yer mama?

PRECIOUS: Better. She watched a rerun of *Captain Kangaroo*. She sang when Bunny Rabbit pawed the alphabet fer Grandfather Clock. She still gits depressed and cries that Mr. Green Jeans is gone.

DWAYNE: When I wuz little, Mama used to tell me I wuz the spittin' image of Mr. Green Jeans. I never did look like Papa.

(BO chokes on coffee.)

PRECIOUS: *(Places finger over lips and mimes, shhh.)* Dwayne Lee? Want me to slice a banana fer yer cereal?

DWAYNE: It's too late, now. I line the banana whirls on the bottom, then add the cereal, then the milk. You know that.

PRECIOUS: Well, it's backwards.

DWAYNE: Well, it's the way I like it.

PRECIOUS: *(Whispers.)* It's still backwards.

DWAYNE: *(Whispers.)* It's still the way I like it.

PRECIOUS: *(Whispers softer.)* It's still backwards.

DWAYNE: *(Whispers softer.)* It's still the way I like it.

(PRECIOUS mouths the words, "It's still backwards," and Dwayne mouths the words, "It's still the way I like it." They do this several times and then PRECIOUS additionally uses her hand to make motions like a mouth is talking. DWAYNE mirrors her motions. They do this back and forth, slowly moving their mouth-hands closer to one another.)

BRENT: *(Enters from outside.)* I forgot my . . .
(Stops to watch DWYANE'S and PRECIOUS' talking hands.)
 . . . my bait . . . That looks better if you shine a flashlight and make shadows on the walls.
(Grabs bait pail and exits outside. Sits on porch.)

(DWYANE'S hand-mouth bites PRECIOUS' hand-mouth.)

PRECIOUS: *(Recoils.)* Ouch! That's 'xactly why you went to jail!

DWAYNE: Nobody goes to jail fer bitin' their sister's hand.

PRECIOUS: Pushin' over a Porta-Johnny with Police Braden inside. Same difference.

DWAYNE: Bo, tell Precious Grace bitin' somebody's hand with yer hand ain't the same thing as Porta-Johnny tippin'.

BO: *(Disinterested.)* Precious, biting someone's hand with your hand ain't the same thing as Porta-Johnny tipping.

PRECIOUS: Well, I don't see no difference.

DWAYNE: Well, you started it.

PRECIOUS: My hand wuz only talkin'.

DWAYNE: So wuz mine.

PRECIOUS: Yer hand bit my hand. I got two witnesses.

DWAYNE: I got two witnesses.

PRECIOUS: Well, I do.

DWAYNE: Well, I do.

> *(PRECIOUS whispers, "Well, I do," as she uses her hand to make motions like a mouth talking. DWAYNE mirrors her motions. They continue but no longer whisper, just make hand-mouths move in silence. They do this back and forth, slowly moving their mouth-hands closer to one another. DWYANE'S hand-mouth again bites PRECIOUS' hand-mouth.)*

PRECIOUS: *(Screams.)* Rape! Rape! Rape!

(DWAYNE quickly sits, thrusts his hands over his ears, and buries his head on the table. PRECIOUS grabs a banana, cuts one slice, and holds the slice between her thumb and finger in the air for all to see. She prances to DWAYNE'S cereal, and in a ceremonial victory, plops the slice on top of his cereal. She proudly struts to sink.)

DWEZEL: Speaking'a the railroad becomin' extinct, when winters is warm, people use less coal. Fewer coal cars is built. That's why railroads shut down car-shop operations. People don't have work. Move away. Less groceries is bought. Why the City-Dump-Street Piggley Wiggley's closin'.

PRECIOUS: That's fascinatin', Uncle Dwezel. Is yer children comin' to Mama's funeral, I mean, *if* Mama dies?

DWEZEL: Well, Annie Mae's youngest youngin' has the chickenpox, so if yer ma dies next week, she'll be able to make it, but if it's this week, she won't.

PRECIOUS: Well, let's hope fer next week. I ain't seen Annie Mae in three years.

DWEZEL: She looks more and more like her ma by the day.

BO: Fat?

DWEZEL: No. Bald. We bought Annie Mae a new wig from Prison Road Mall. Wouldn't wear her ma's wigs. We buried her ma in her favorite wig, Shirley Temple twirls. Don't think she'd a minded Annie Mae wearin' one'a her beehive or Loretta-Lynn-style wigs. Would'a saved us nineteen dollar.
(Takes a bite of cereal and suddenly stops chewing.)
Dad blame it!
(Hurries to sink and holds up his dentures to examine.)

41

PRECIOUS: What's the matter, Uncle Dwezel? Oat bran jammed in yer dentures agin?

DWEZEL: Last time I buy a used pair of dentures from Tancy Grace's Flea Market.

BO: God Almighty! Doesn't anybody in this family ever discuss important things?

PRECIOUS: Like what?

BO: The news. The news. You know? The News. What's going on in the world!

PRECIOUS: Well, Bo, what's going on in the world?

DWAYNE: What happened, Bo? What is it?

(BRENT enters from porch as BERTHA enters from upstairs.)

BERTHA: What's all the pandemonium down here?

PRECIOUS: Somethin' awful happened!

DWAYNE: Bo wuz jest about to tell us the news.

BERTHA: Oh, no. It's not Mama, is it?

PRECIOUS: No, no. It's the world!

BERTHA: The world! Oh, no, Bo. What is it?

PRECIOUS: Go on, Bo, tell us.

BO: Uh . . . uh . . .
(Carelessly looks at first page of his newspaper and reads.)

"First lady tells women of China to stand up for their rights."

DWEZEL: Speakin' 'bout the way buses' hydraulic brakes work, one didn't stop and squashed Gladys Fitches' poodle puppy.

PRECIOUS: Oh, heavens! Why didn't Gladys have her poodle puppy on a leash?

DWEZEL: She did. Wuz tied to her wheelchair. The bus snatched up that poodle puppy and towed Gladys clear down past Buddy's Amoco.

BRENT: A world news story, a local news story.

BO: Okay, here!
(Looks at newspaper.)
"Croatians and Serbians accused of enslaving one another."

DWAYNE: What's a Cro-station?

DWEZEL: Gladys wouldn't'a been hurt neither, if she ain't been towed through Elmira Gleason's prize-winnin' yellow roses. Got thirteen thorns embedded in her bosoms. Doc Pendergas had to lance'em out under general anesthesia.

PRECIOUS: You'd think Gladys learnt her lesson last summer when Hell's Angels rode through and big Boomer Dog wuz tied to her hammock. Bo?

BO: Don't bother. I don't want to know!

PRECIOUS: How you gonna git educated if you don't keep up with the news?

BO: I'm going to take a nap.

BRENT: You just woke up, dude

BO: *(Grabs BRENT by the shoulders and puts his face in BRENT'S face.)* Are you sure about that? Absolutely, positively sure about that? I've been in this dream for decades, and if I could wake up, I would!
(Exits upstairs.)

BRENT: That dude's got to be on something that's not even made it to the West Coast.

DWAYNE: You can't photograph women in underwear all day and not git a little subnormal.

BRENT: Yeah, dudes. That's gotta be too much excellence for one mind.
(Exits outside and off stage.)

DWEZEL: Speakin'a bison made me remember. I gotta run to the store fer yer ma. Promised her I'd pick up some whip cream and more Red Man.
(Exits to outside and leaves stage.)

PRECIOUS: *(Yells.)* I'll tell Mama to savor the chew in her mouth 'til you git back.

BERTHA: Precious, what on earth are you going to do when Mama's gone?

DWAYNE: Whew!
(Abruptly stands.)
I'll be at Buddy's.

PRECIOUS: You want more oat bran?

DWAYNE: No thank you.

PRECIOUS: More two-percent?

DWAYNE: No thank you, Precious. Tell Mama I'll be back. *(Exits to outside and leaves stage.)*

PRECIOUS: *(Yells.)* Don't drink none! . . . I worry 'bout his liver.

BERTHA: Does Dwayne come around often?

PRECIOUS: Not since him and Sue Jean separated. He jest kind'a hangs out at Buddy's. Drinks. I think bein' in jail sucked the wind outta him. Remember how him and Hoy, and Troy Cox, and Dawson Redpath used to cut up all the time? He don't give'em the time'a day. Thinks them boys won't think he's a man no more, not since what happened to him sharin' that jail cell with that big trucker fella. Stripped poor Dwayne's manhood clean off'im. When he first got outta jail, he slept with his door locked. Leaned a chair against it, in case the lock broke. I heard him cry the hidin'-yer-face-in-the-pillow kind'a cryin'. He won't touch Sue Jean. That's why she left'im. She only made it up Dwayne flirted with Bobby Rose so Dwayne could feel more man-like.

BERTHA: So, what will you do with yourself? When Mama's gone?

PRECIOUS: *(Alarmed.)* Gone!

BERTHA: When she dies.

PRECIOUS: Oh, I thought you meant she was leavin'. She's jest dyin', Bertha Sue.

BERTHA: But she'll be gone.

PRECIOUS: She can't help dyin'! She'll be up on Hawk's Hill. Next to Papa. Grandpa and Grandma Beecher. Great Granny Blossom.

BERTHA: Who will shop for you? You stay stuck in this house.

PRECIOUS: I walk up Hawk's Hill every Sunday. A course, I don't go near no woods. I steer clear'a all woods. Too much bad there.

BERTHA: Like what?

PRECIOUS: Things. Things you won't see, but all the same, you know is there, watchin'.

BERTHA: Who'll drive you to the doctor?

PRECIOUS: I don't need no doctor! I don't know what gives you and Bo the right to come home and act like I'm stupid!

BERTHA: I didn't mean it to sound that way . . . Sometimes, I miss this place awful. Everyone knowing everyone. Beginnings and endings clear as a bell. Other times I don't want to remember any of it.

PRECIOUS: Bertha Sue Reamy, or whatever yer last name is now. What did anybody here ever do to you that was so terrible?

BERTHA: Just seems like these mountains, the schools, something holds me down.

PRECIOUS: Well, you live way off in Californie now. Do what you please.

BERTHA: People carry old baggage long distances. Can't just leave it at the Greyhound station.

PRECIOUS: Mama and Papa sent you off with the most beautiful embroidered bags I ever seen. Stitches with love in every hole and thread. Big pastel flowers.

BERTHA: I keep missing something.

PRECIOUS: Figure out what it is.

BERTHA: I spent a fortune and four husbands trying.

PRECIOUS: Close yer eyes.

BERTHA: What?

PRECIOUS: Mama plays this game when I git moody.

BERTHA: Oh.

(Both close their eyes.)

PRECIOUS: Think of a moment when you felt good.

BERTHA: Uh huh.

PRECIOUS: What is it?

BERTHA: A big church in LA. Wilshire Christian.

PRECIOUS: Oooh. I see it, Bertha Sue.

BERTHA: Church has an old piano. I sneaked in and played it. Whatever came to my fingers. As I left, there was an old woman by the doors. Wrinkled face. Gray hair in a simple scarf. She shook my hand and smiled this partial-toothed smile.

PRECIOUS: I see her. Oh! I know what yer missin'!

BERTHA: You do?

47

PRECIOUS: People hearin' yer music!

(Both open their eyes.)

BERTHA: I never wanted people to hear my music.

PRECIOUS: Eleventh grade? Concert Band? You said you wanted to knock off ole Mr. Irv Bob.

BERTHA: Irving Bobzinkichoff—or something—the Jewish band director who moved here from New York.

PRECIOUS: You wanted to be the conductor.

BERTHA: That piece of music we played when we won the state championship. I dreamed of standing on the podium, all those instruments, all eyes looking straight at me. And take up the baton. I told Izetta Flowers. *She* told everybody, "No girl from Brantley Run should want to do a tacky thing like conduct." That's when Woodrow Willis Woodburn told me he knew a baton I would enjoy holding lots more than a band conductor's baton. I was stupid enough to go to the Thundercloud Drive-In with him and make out in his dirty old Volkswagen bus.

PRECIOUS: We still have yer old band record. Mama keeps it right beside old Blue Eyes' best.

BERTHA: She does not!

PRECIOUS: Lookie right here.
(Walks to cabinet, gets record, and places it on the turntable.)

BERTHA: Mama never liked music.

PRECIOUS: 'Cause she's tone deaf.

BERTHA: It won't sound as good as I remember.

PRECIOUS: State champeens.
(Plays the record. The sound is, "Fantasia on 'The 'Dargason'" from the <u>Second Suite in F, Op. 28, No. 2 by Gustav Holst</u>.)

BERTHA: The Second Suit. Oh, my gosh.

PRECIOUS: Do it.

BERTHA: I was third clarinet. Jojo and Dede on my right, Jayjay, Kaykay, and Bobo on my left.

PRECIOUS: Conduct'em.

BERTHA: Yates Weston was on tympani, looking handsome as a soldier.

PRECIOUS: They's waitin' fer you.

BERTHA: We had formal dresses, so our clarinets had to be held to the side. Very lady-like.

PRECIOUS: *(Slides a chair to Bertha and pats it.)* Yer podium. Conduct.

BERTHA: Precious, you're making me feel silly.

(PRECIOUS hands a large turkey baster to BERTHA. BERTHA looks around to assure no one is watching, stands on the chair, and conducts, moving the turkey baster to the music.)

PRECIOUS: Yer doin' it!
(She is a delighted child, swaying her head as if playing an instrument.)

(BERTHA conducts with great enthusiasm, eventually closing her eyes.)

(Slowly, BO, DWAYNE, DWEZEL, BRENT, EULA, and TODD enter the kitchen. BERTHA is lost in conducting, seeing no one until she opens her eyes and abruptly realizes people are staring. She screams and covers her face with embarrassment. TODD lifts BERTHA from her chair and swings her around. PRECIOUS turns off the record player.)

BERTHA: I was conducting my old band.

PRECIOUS: And she won!

BERTHA: Well, state champions.

BRENT: Mom, someone must have like totally spiked your well water.

BERTHA: Just coming home.

(TODD grabs BERTHA by her hand and hurriedly pulls her upstairs.)

DWEZEL: Speakin'a New Zealand, I took yer advice, Bo, caught up on world news. Got myself one'a them international newspapers at Rock and Dots. It's got a story about two boys right cheer from Brantley Run.

EULA: No! Who?

DWEZEL: Bubba Limley and J.T. Habber.

PRECIOUS: Bubba Limley and J.T. Habber?

DWEZEL: Last month, they gone skiin' in New Zealand. Waved at two purty girls. Climbed onto a chair lift. Half-way up the mountain, this little green patch'a fog enveloped'em fer a few seconds. When the chairs come outta the green fog, Bubba . . . and one'a the girls . . . *Disappeared!* Et up by the fog.

PRECIOUS: That's too tragic to repeat!

BO: Oh, come on!

(DWEZEL holds up tabloid newspaper.)

BO: That . . . That's a tabloid, Uncle Dwezel. Those aren't news stories.

DWEZEL: Wrote in newsprint. Got a picture'a the chairlift and everythin'. Artist's rendition.

BO: There's probably not even a Bubba Limley and J.T. Habber from Brantley Run.

PRECIOUS: I never heard of'em.

DWEZEL: Makes it even stranger. Never git me in no chairlift.

EULA: Me neither, Dwezel.

BO: I swear.

EULA: Bo Ray Reamy! Don't be a swearin' in yer mama's house.

BO: I wasn't swearing like swearing. It's an expression, like, "I swanee."

EULA: Well, say, "I swanee."

DWEZEL: Speakin'a the recession, Police Chief Skyler said the Brantley Run Police budget is tight, so after

Sergeant Hopper totaled his police car, Hopper's gotta do all future police work on a bicycle.

(BERTHA enters from upstairs, self-conscious and straightening her clothes and hair, obviously after super quick, passionate sex.)

PRECIOUS: Hopper already made one arrest on his bicycle. Chased down an eighteen-wheeler. The driver said he only stopped 'cause he thought it was a joke.

DWAYNE: Hopper lost seventy-four pounds peddlin' that bike.

BERTHA: Bo, tell that story Mama used to tell every time we visited Uncle Arthur in South Carolina.

BO: I don't know, Bertha. I haven't heard that story in a long time.

PRECIOUS: You mean crazy Harold? Oh, Mama loves that story. Only, she gits a bit on the tear-side'a things when she tells it. Well, Mama grew up in South Carolina, outside'a Dillon. There wuz this crazy growed boy named, Harold. He didn't have no car, jest a steerin' wheel, and he parked it downtown, jest like most anybody, only he parked his steerin' wheel. Then, everybody knowed not to park there. One day, crazy Harold had drove onto the railroad tracks, and his car stalled, right smack on the tracks.

BRENT: You mean his steering wheel stalled?

PRECIOUS: Uh huh. The train wuz comin'. Everybody heard it. The tracks run plum through the center'a town, so everybody seen poor crazy Harold out on the tracks, doin' his darndest to start his car.

BRENT: His steering wheel.

PRECIOUS: Uh huh. Everybody yelled as loud as they could fer crazy Harold to leave his car. The train killt him.

BRENT: No!

PRECIOUS: Grandma Beecher covered Mama's eyes.

BRENT: That's wrong, man. He could have been grabbed.

PRECIOUS: Crazy Harold couldn't be grabbed, Brent honey. He wuz in his car. That's Mama's favorite story.

DWAYNE: Papa used to love Mama tellin' that story. He promised he wuz gonna git it published in *Field and Stream.*

(Sound of loud TV voices with rapidly changing channels.)

PRECIOUS: I swan 'de goodness! Somebody let Mama near the remote control agin!
(Exits upstairs.)

BERTHA: Hearing Precious tell stories, it's just like Mama and Papa, and Grandma, and Great Granny Blossom are all sitting right here. She keeps them alive.

DWAYNE: Hell, she talks to each of'em ev'ry night. Blessin'em and tellin'em jokes and singin' with'em. Ev'ry once in a while she tries to feed'em.

BERTHA: Oh Dwayne, Precious Grace is so happy here. And you're her best friend. Isn't he, Bo?

BO: Yep.

DWAYNE: Oh, no. You two ain't ropin' me into takin' care'a Precious Grace. Uh uh.

BERTHA: You're right here close by. You don't have to do much. Sign a guardianship paper that—

DWAYNE: Uh uh.

BO: Come on, Dwayne. Do it for Papa. He would have wanted you to be Precious Grace's guardian.

DWAYNE: Papa never used to take me huntin', or shoot hoops, or swimmin'. Buddies' daddy always done them things with *him*. Skinny-dippin' in Glady Creek. Papa never went.

BO: I doubt Papa was much for skinny-dipping. He built you that basketball court.

DWAYNE: A dirt court!

BO: A tree house, a swing.

BERTHA: Oh, I loved that swing. Papa did lots for you.

BO: Don't bad talk Papa. You haven't stood in his shoes.

DWAYNE: What makes you an expert on Papa?

BO: Talk to Precious about Papa. She's the expert.

DWAYNE: Precious Grace is loco. You know what she said about Papa and Mama?

BO: I'm afraid to imagine.

DWAYNE: She said Papa and Mama never got married.

BERTHA: Oh, for crying out loud, Dwayne.

DWAYNE: I went down to the courthouse and looked it up so's I could win five dollar off Precious. I couldn't find no record of 'em marryin' nowheres.

EULA: Dwayne Lee Reamy!
(Beats on DWAYNE with her church paper fan.)
You got no business pryin' into other people's affairs. They got four good-lookin' kids, which fer them weren't no easy feat to accomplish. Four children, who ought to have the decency to be thankful that them hard-workin', God-fearin' two people put a roof over yer heads, and filled yer bellies, and most'a all, filled you little kids up with manners and love. I'm sure not seein' no results'a all that in this conversation.

DWAYNE: No ma'am, Aunt Eula, I didn't say I didn't appreciate 'em. I jest hinted they wuz . . . unusual.

EULA: They wuz ahead'a their time.

BO: A few zillion, jillion years.

BERTHA: Ahead of their time?
(Laughs loudly.)

EULA: Never mind, Bertha Sue. Go chase men all over California.

BERTHA: Pardon me, Aunt Eula. That was real unkind.

PRECIOUS: *(Storms down steps.)* Dwayne Lee Reamy! Did you git Mama to give you four-hundred dollar out'a my pot'a gold?

DWAYNE: Mama forced that money on me.

PRECIOUS: Mama don't force no money on nobody, least'a all you!

BERTHA: Oh, Dwayne, give Precious back her money.

DWAYNE: Mama give it to me.

BERTHA: Precious has been saving that money most of her life.

PRECIOUS: Give it back, Dwayne Lee.

DWAYNE: It's mine!

BO: *(Pulls out his wallet.)* Here, Dwayne. I'll give you four-hundred dollars.

DWAYNE: No! It's from Mama. She give it to me.

PRECIOUS: Fer what?

DWAYNE: I can't say.

PRECIOUS: Fer what?

DWAYNE: It's a secret between me and Mama.

PRECIOUS: Mama don't make no secrets with you. You fooled her outta that money.

DWAYNE: I did not.

PRECIOUS: Is it fer booze?

DWAYNE: Precious! That's unfair.

PRECIOUS: Is it to bail that Buddy outta some legal misdemeanor agin?

DWAYNE: Buddy is my best friend, Precious. You wouldn't know what that means, would you? You ain't got no friends.

(EULA hits DWAYNE with her fan.)

PRECIOUS: I would rather not have no friends than to hang around with a poor excuse like Buddy.

BERTHA: Precious, Dwayne, can we stop this?

DWAYNE: Buddy is one of the finest people who ever walked Brantley Run.

PRECIOUS: That's not the trash I heard from Buddy's grandma's own lips. If it didn't make me appear tacky to repeat it, I would. But the Reamy name is much too much of a treasure to tarnish.

(TODD enters from upstairs, wearing skimpy California beach wear with no shirt. He carries a beach chair and classic-bound leather book. He walks across the kitchen without eye contact, spits in the sink, walks to the refrigerator, and gulps from a bottle of orange juice. He places the bottle back into the refrigerator without the lid, pats his stomach, belches, leaves the refrigerator door open, and exits to the porch. He sits in his chair and reads his book. Throughout TODD'S movements, the others stare silently, their heads moving together as if watching a tennis match. Some may have to turn awkwardly in their seats or stand and strain to watch him.)

DWAYNE: Next time you—any of you—call my friend Buddy trash, think about it hard.
(He slams shut the refrigerator door.)

PRECIOUS: I don't mean nothin' by it. It's jest that Buddy drinks and gits you drinkin'.

DWAYNE: After that bus-drivin' accident, after that little Thompson girl didn't walk out far enough in front'a

Buddy's bus? Wouldn't nobody speak to him. He'd drove that bus fer six years, then they all acted like he run down a little girl on purpose. Buddy has nightmares can't nobody shake. A little beer makes'em go away. Any of you know what it's like to have nightmares, over and over? I do.

PRECIOUS: I said, I'm sorry.

DWAYNE: Don't act so uppity.

BERTHA: People aren't uppity just because they don't like you drinking yourself into the grave.

DWAYNE: Some people talk real nice, say, "I wish you and Buddy would stop drinkin'," like old lady Hendricks. 'Cause she cares. Other people use the same words but say it uppity. "I wish you would stop drinkin'!" 'Cause they want to feel they's better than you.

PRECIOUS: That's one'a Mama's sayin's.

DWAYNE: Sayin's. That's all I got from that contrary woman.

PRECIOUS: Dwayne Lee Reamy!

DWAYNE: She give me this four-hundred dollar, then you know what she told me?

BO: Can imagine.

DWAYNE: "Dwayne Lee darlin', I sure hope you don't end up killin' and rapin' people." I says to her, "Mama, I got too much good from you and Papa to ever do bad." Mama said, "Yer papa wuz jest a little short thug with four tattoos and a hard-criminal stare that could melt the dial off a bank vault." Then she passed out.

BO: Nope. I did not see that coming.

DWAYNE: Our papa didn't have no four tattoos.

PRECIOUS: Well Dwayne Lee, *yer* papa weren't really—

BO: Precious! Why don't you check on Mama?

BERTHA: Mama's stories sound like she's getting delirious. I'll check on her.
(Exits upstairs.)

EULA: One time, we had two US government geneologist folk sent down here. Wanted to draw family trees on everybody in Brantley Run. Well, those two wet-behind-the-ears, over-educated fellers drew their little lines and circles, criss-crossin'em this way and that. Finally, one of'em said, "Anybody who ever tried to decipher the history and lineage of the Carroll Lynn Reamy family, had a task the size of translatin' the Dead Sea Scrolls. They wuz never seen agin in Brantley Run.

(All laugh with pleasure.)

BERTHA: *(Runs down the steps, out of breath, with hands over her chest.)* Mama's not breathing.

(DWAYNE and BO run upstairs as TODD hurries in from the porch and hugs BERTHA. BRENT hurries outside and sits on the porch, frightened, occasionally glancing through the window.)

EULA: *(Sits and clutches her shopping bag dearly, as if it is the last thing in life she has to hug, rocking back and forth and mumbling to herself, interspersed with humming a hymn.)* Oh Lordy, Lordy. Oh, Lordy, Lordy.

PRECIOUS: Okay now. Where's that stuff Mama wrote fer when this wuz to happen? Anybody seen Mama's little brown notebook?
(Panics as she searches drawers and shelves, spilling items onto the floor.)

DWAYNE: *(Enters from upstairs.)* Will somebody call Doc Pendergas fer God's sake? Mama's dyin'!
(Exits upstairs.)

DWEZEL: *(Walks to phone and dials.)* Is Doc there? This is Dwezel Beecher . . . Doc? My sister's dyin' . . . Yes, sir. *(Pause.)*
Yes, sir. Thank you kindly.
(Hangs up phone and sits, arms propped on his knees to brace himself, motionless.)

PRECIOUS: *(Finds notebook.)* Oh, thank goodness.
(Thumbs to a page and reads.)
"Number one: Call the Zucarri Funeral Home. Number two: Remind Mr. Sledge the casket has already been selected and paid fer. Number three: If Mr. Sledge fergits, remind him, it's the number-806-style, plain-wooden casket. Don't let him talk the family into nothin' else. Number four—"

(DWAYNE enters and slumps against the wall. BO slowly enters, stopping on the bottom steps. Pauses. Everyone, except DWAYNE, turns and stares motionlessly at BO.)

BO: *(Pauses a long time before speaking.)* Mama's gone.

(EULA resumes singing hymn.)

PRECIOUS: *(Resumes reading.)* "Number four: Call Iva Dean to arrange flowers fer church. Number five: Call Lucy Mae to arrange flowers fer cemetery. Let them both know Mama likes both their floral arrangements and cannot pick jest one of em. Number six—"

(Looks at ceiling, hallucinating, stands and screams.)
Not now! Later!

(Others freeze in horror and stare at PRECIOUS.)

PRECIOUS: *(Sits, looks at notebook, and reads calmly as if nothing happened.)* "Number six: Call Lib at Piggly Wiggly to prepare the hors-d'oeuvres tray. Number seven—"

(The lights go down to black.)

ACT THREE

LATE AFTERNOON IN THE KITCHEN

BO, BERTHA, and DWAYNE are sitting at the table, making banana splits. PRECIOUS races around the kitchen, serving whatever the others demand.

BERTHA: Pass the caramel topping. I don't think the Zucarri Funeral Home could have made Mama look any more natural.

BO: Pass the fudge topping. I've never seen a funeral home make a dead person grin like that.

PRECIOUS: Mr. Sledge hired a new boy to do the mouths. He ain't got the hang of it. Anybody want strawberries?

DWAYNE: Me.

PRECIOUS: Do you think Mama minds we're eating all this ice cream without blessin' it?

DWAYNE: Well, Precious Grace, it ain't exactly a full-course meal.

BERTHA: Well, I for one, will never forgive Uncle Dwezel for such poor timing. Walk up during the opening prayer, give Mama a farewell kiss on the lips, everyone watching, and die.

DWAYNE: The five minutes Dwezel wuz bent over her casket, his lips on Mama's lips? I jest thought it wuz an awful long brother-sister kiss.

PRECIOUS: I knowed somethin' weren't right when he didn't stand fer, "How Firm a Foundation." That wuz his favorite hymn.

BERTHA: Well, Mama and Dwezel are together again.

BO: They were only apart forty-eight hours.

PRECIOUS: Bo, that was real nice how Sumter and the boys come up fer Mama's funeral. Too bad they couldn't stay a day longer fer Dwezel's.

BO: Sumter took over planning a neighbor girl's debutante ball. That's chocolate topping; I wanted fudge.

DWAYNE: Wild Aunt Eula went off her trolley like that.

PRECIOUS: Well, when you take away people's cookies, Bo, people git bedeviled.

BO: There's no way curtailing Eula from a few Stelazine cookies made her steal Police Chief Skyler's hood ornament.

PRECIOUS: She looked real pathetic bein' shackled, carted off to a psych hospital.

BERTHA: Weston'll take good care of her. Anyone get her key for the freezer padlock?

BO: She had the death grip on it. You'd have to chop her hand off.

BERTHA: I couldn't get over how many people knew and respected Mama. There must have been two hundred people there.

DWAYNE: Hundred fourteen. Let me have a cherry.

BERTHA: There was this one man standing on the edge of the cemetery—

PRECIOUS: In a ragged coat with elbow patches? I seen him. He looked trashy.

BERTHA: Sam something or other. He came up from Dillon. Aunt Gypsy Branch told him about Mama's death. He said when he was little, working in the Dillon Mill, his family didn't have lunch money. Mama was just sixteen, but she packed two lunches every day for Dwezel, so he could slip one into Sam's locker. Drove all the way from South Carolina for Mama.

DWAYNE: And fer Dwezel. Can I please have a cherry?

PRECIOUS: You put the cherry on after the whip cream.

DWAYNE: I put it on first.

BO: Then it gets buried under the whip cream.

DWAYNE: Where I like it.

BERTHA: Nobody buries their cherry under their whip cream.

PRECIOUS: Mama always said when you wuz teethin' she give you too much paregoric. That's why she called you, her little opium-head.

DWAYNE: She never called me her little opium-head.

PRECIOUS: *Put* the cherry under the cream. Mama's where she can see you now.

BERTHA: Hope she can't see what I'll be doing.

PRECIOUS: Don't matter if you close the bedroom door, Bertha Sue. Mama's in heaven now.

BO: For gosh sakes. Sumter and I spent four years in sex therapy getting comfortable without a heavy quilt hiding us from the sky. Now, you have me paranoid Mama's watching between the bed posts.

DWAYNE: You know that little knot-hole behind the linen closet bottom shelf?

BERTHA: Next to the attic bedroom? Sure do.

DWAYNE: One time, I wuz in the attic bedroom, after workin' out, lookin' at my muscles in Aunt Catherine Gracie's dressin' mirror. I weren't wearin' nothin'.

PRECIOUS: Oh, my!

DWAYNE: I seen this eyeball peepin' through that knot-hole. Mama's.

BO: No!

BERTHA: You were always showing off naked in front of that old mirror.

DWAYNE: Uh uh!

BERTHA: Rowena Jellicourse and I watched you a dozen times.

DWAYNE: Through the knot hole? Perverts!

PRECIOUS: Anybody like pineapple or butterscotch toppin'? On *top*'a their whip cream?

BO: Yes, please.

BERTHA: Rowena said, when she got married, she expected Colonel Hoyt to pose for her, like you. Disappointed he never did. Of course, he wasn't you. He was flabby!

DWAYNE: Think I still got the look?
(Stands and poses.)

PRECIOUS: Dwayne Lee? Yer still a handsome, lovin'-lookin' guy. Sue Jean said so, when she brung ginger roots. Said she seen you at Buddy's Amoco, standin' at the grease rack, yer arms stretched way up high—

DWAYNE: I got a sudden hankerin' fer air.
(Hurriedly exits onto porch and leaves the stage.)

PRECIOUS: *(Yells.)* She wants you back, Dwayne! She don't mind what happened to you. The children want you back, too, Dwayne!

BERTHA: Let him go, Precious.

PRECIOUS: Little Dwayne Junior said so, real pitiful like.
(Walks across the kitchen with a marked limp.)

BERTHA: Why Precious Grace, what happened to your leg?

PRECIOUS: Not a thing, Bertha Sue.

BERTHA: You're limping big as all get out. You look like Mama trying to hobble through Piggley Wiggley with her arthritis.

PRECIOUS: It's jest fine, Bertha Sue.

BERTHA: That ain't "just fine."

PRECIOUS: I got too much to do, to worry about who does or don't have arthritis.

BERTHA: Since when do you have arthritis?

PRECIOUS: Since standin' in rain fer three hours singin' hymns on top'a Hawk's Hill. *Twiced!* We could'a waited 'til a sunny day.

BERTHA: You can't hold funerals for the sun.

PRECIOUS: I put everybody's favorite quilt on their bed. Even Dwayne Lee's. He slept here last night. First time in a year. Not countin' one little dram-drunk episode.

BO: Doll baby, we'll all be leaving.

PRECIOUS: Mama would love this, eatin' ice-cream, talkin'—

BERTHA: Todd, uh, Brent, and I, we're scheduled to fly out tonight.

PRECIOUS: Tonight?

BERTHA: Mr. Milrose is giving us a ride up to Pittsburgh.

PRECIOUS: That'll be lonesome-like, jest Dwayne Lee and Bo.

BERTHA: Well . . . I need to pack a few things. *(Exits upstairs.)*

BO: *(Leads PRECIOUS out to the porch.)* At Uncle Dwezel's funeral, I talked with Foster Pendle. He said how nice you looked.

PRECIOUS: He did not.

BO: Stood right there on Hawk's Hill and said, "That Precious Grace Reamy is a knockout in her funeral dress."

PRECIOUS: Foster Pendle ain't been grounded since they pried an ax outta his skull.

BO: Foster's not the only man in Brantley Run to give you a second look.

PRECIOUS: No one's gonna date me. I ain't never even been asked to no dance before.

BO: In high school?

PRECIOUS: Let Bertha Sue dream about fancy Californie pin-up men. I'm stuck here listenin' to Verna Mae sit back on her stories'a tap and charm school, memories'a high school graduation, dancin' with the quarterback, Mike Roton. "He put his arm 'round my waist. We moved through space, the record player whinin' a colored man's saxophone. That sexy sax slid up real high, and Mike squeezed my hand real tight." Nobody asked me to dance. Papa bought me my corsage. Remember how Great Granny Blossom used to bake ginger rolls at Thanksgivin'? Tonight, I'll fix ginger rolls. Havin' you and Dwayne Lee home is kind'a like Thanksgivin'. Or sweet potato pie?

BO: Either. Both.

(PRECIOUS returns to the kitchen and BO follows.)

PRECIOUS: Hope I got ginger root. If Eula didn't git into our spices 'fore they drug her off.

BO: She'll be fine . . . The old Patwitty Farm sold for three-hundred thousand dollars.

PRECIOUS: That little ole thing?

BO: To build the last bit of a golf course.

PRECIOUS: Who in Brantley Run hits golf balls?

BO: People don't always farm. People ski, snowboard, stay in condominiums.

PRECIOUS: People gotta farm if they wanna eat.

BRENT: *(Enters from upstairs.)* Mom said we're leaving.

PRECIOUS: You'll miss Thanksgivin' dinner. Creamy macaroni with stewed tomaters, tomater aspic, fried deer burgers, watercress carefully picked outta Dwezel's creek—God bless his soul—And? My own private blend'a ginger rolls.

BRENT: Weird Thanksgiving spread, Precious Grace. Not to mention, it's August.

(BRENT exits to porch and sits. PRECIOUS follows. BO remains inside and reads.)

PRECIOUS: I read in the encyclopedia that Christmas really ain't even at Christmas. The Romans moved the calendar plum around.

BRENT: We don't celebrate Christmas either.

PRECIOUS: Don't . . . Don't celebrate Christmas?

BRENT: Nope. I mean, no ma'am. Mom says while we're here if I can learn to say, "fix breakfast," and "mash the button," and "cut off the light," I "might could" learn to say, "no ma'am" and "yes ma'am."

PRECIOUS: Right on, dude! Now did you take seven teaspoons'a canned blackberries like I pre-scribed?

BRENT: They stopped my runs all right. I haven't been able to dump, I mean . . . have a bowel movement since.

PRECIOUS: That's jest way too many canned blackberries fer a human yer size. Tell you what. On the dresser, next to Mama's Nintendo, is a jar of pinto-bean extract. *(Pulls a measuring spoon from her apron pocket.)* Take two tablespoons, definitely no more, but don't go near Mama's pillow! You might could set off her pistol.

BRENT: *Pistol?*

BO: *(Hears through screen window.)* No one got rid of Mama's . . . That killing instrument could go off! *(Hurriedly exits upstairs.)*

PRECIOUS: So, if you don't celebrate Christmas, what do you do?

BRENT: Go to Starfighter Theme Park.

PRECIOUS: What do you do there?

BRENT: Ride starfighter mountain.

PRECIOUS: What's that?

BRENT: Like a roller-coaster, but in a dark cave.

PRECIOUS: Wouldn't git me in there.

BRENT: It's excellent. Totally excellent.

PRECIOUS: Not fer no million dollar.

BRENT: You go up and down and around and eject really fast out this long tunnel!

PRECIOUS: Uh uh! Never!

BRENT: Makes you feel like you're going upside down and tilting over!

PRECIOUS: No, no.

BRENT: Have your blood sucked up into your head and explode out your eyeballs!

PRECIOUS: Gross!

BRENT: Isn't it? Okay, okay. Sit here.
(Motions for PRECIOUS to sit on chair or swing next to him.)

PRECIOUS: What are we doin'?

BRENT: Be quiet. Real quiet. You and I are going into starfighter mountain.

PRECIOUS: Oh, no, no!

BRENT: Just pretend. It's like totally cool.

PRECIOUS: Well, if it's only pretend. But you better not really send me into no starfighter mountain. My heart won't handle it.

BRENT: No heart ailments or short kids past the loading platform. Okay, okay. Buckle up.

(PRECIOUS stares at BRENT as he pretends to buckle up.)

BRENT: *(Looks at her.)* What's your problem, lady? You going to ride this starship nude? Buckle up.

PRECIOUS: Oh, gosh!
(Pretends to buckle up.)

71

BRENT: Like a pro!
(Uses the measuring spoon as his microphone.)
"Space platform to launch pad." Our car's easing up the red launch megatube. Chug, chug, chug. "All starfighters prepare for blast-off." Lean back, we're aiming up at the infinities.

(They lean back.)

BRENT: "Are all space travelers locked in?" Check your belt.

(They look at their belts in parallel moves.)

BRENT: "We're ready fleet commander." Hang on. Five . . . four . . . This is going to be a lot of G's, dude. Three . . . two . . . one . . . Here we go . . . *Blast-off.* Zzzzzzsssss.

(BRENT presses his body back deeply into chair/swing. PRECIOUS watches him and imitates everything he does, screaming loudly and giggling as they play. They lean left, down, forward, and backward according to what BRENT calls out and does.)

BRENT: Up . . . up . . . up . . . *left* turn . . . Round . . . round . . . round . . . *right* turn! Round . . . round . . . round . . . *down*! *Up*!

PRECIOUS: *(Yells.)* Stop, stop! I'm gonna wet my pants!

BRENT: 'Nother *left* turn . . . clang, clang, clang, *bigger* left turn! Oh no, space lasers! Zap, zap, zap.

(BRENT ducks several times and PRECIOUS imitates him.)

PRECIOUS: What's happenin'?

BRENT: Plasma bolts.

PRECIOUS: Plasma bolts? Fire back!

BRENT: Okay crew, you heard the little lady. Fire back!

(BRENT pretends to push his gun button and PRECIOUS imitates him, including making "phhhhhh" and other gun sounds.)

BRENT: Fire one! Phhhhhh! Fire two! Phhhhhh! Fire three. Phhhhhh!

PRECIOUS: I got one!
(Stops for BRENT to admire her actions.)

BRENT: Don't stop! Never stop! The droids are behind us!

PRECIOUS: Oh, my gosh. Git outta here!

BRENT: Believe me, I'm trying!

PRECIOUS: *(Stops playing, stands, stares at porch ceiling, and yells.)* Not now! Later! Can't you see we got droids and plasma bolts to contend with?

(BRENT stops and stares at PRECIOUS.)

PRECIOUS: *(Waves off voices, sits, and resumes fighting with her eyes squinted and concentrating on targets.)* Target four. Phhhhh. Target five. Phhhh.

BRENT: Holy Jerusalem! The lady's got the dark force with her.
(Resumes firing, pointing out targets for them both to gun down.)
There's one. Fire! There's another. Good shot. Coming up on your backside, give it a warp shot!

PRECIOUS: Phhhh ping!

BRENT: All right! Now you're toasting. Phhhh! Control to fighter, control to fighter. This is fighter squadron "J" as in uh . . . "Jaybob." Do you read me, control? "We read you, Jaybob. We've got you sequenced for landing platform beta. Do you read?" We read you, control, and am locking our landing beam for beta. Okay, okay, stop firing. We're secure now.

PRECIOUS: One more renegade fighter off the radar, commander!
(Fires machine gun briefly, making machine gun sounds.)
Ratta tat tat tat tat tat tat tat!

BRENT: Okay, that's enough! You're going to get us booted out by the Supreme Intergalactic Police.

PRECIOUS: It wuz jest one more little—
(Sneaks another quieter shot.)
Phhhh.
(Whispers.)
Got it.

BRENT: Okay. Prepare to touch down.

(BRENT leans far back in seat and squints due to G forces. PRECIOUS imitates him.)

BRENT: *(Throws up arms.)* Touchdown!

PRECIOUS: *(Throws up arms.)* Touchdown!

BRENT: Give me five!
(Holds out the palm of his hand.)

PRECIOUS: *(Slaps his hand.)* Give me five!

(PRECIOUS holds out the palm of her hand. BRENT slaps her hand and PRECIOUS tries to hug him. BRENT jumps back, stares at his hand, and wipes it off on his pants. PRECIOUS turns away, embarrassed.)

BRENT: *(Pauses, embarrassed.)* Miss . . .
(Clears throat.)
Miss Precious Grace . . . I thought it would be more . . . more lady like, ma'am . . . if we shook hands.

PRECIOUS: Oh? Oh! Why a course.

(BRENT pauses, stares at PRECIOUS' hands, and then slowly extends his hand.)

PRECIOUS: Why thank you kindly, Captain Starfighter.
(Hesitantly and weakly shakes hands, and then screams, breaking handclasp and jumping up and down.)
Ahhhhhh! That was *so* excellent!

(They enter the kitchen, laughing as BO and BERTHA enter from upstairs. BERTHA is carrying her designer shopping bag and purse.)

BRENT: Wait 'til we go into the haunted house!

PRECIOUS: Oh, no, no, no!

(BRENT walks to stairs, but when he sees BO and BERTHA, he becomes reserved and exits upstairs.)

PRECIOUS: Did you see where that good-lookin' nephew'a mine took me? Wednesday night church bingo ain't never gonna be the same!

BERTHA: Well, Precious . . . Brent and I would love to have you visit us in California.

PRECIOUS: We got ginger rolls, tonight. Can't understand why you can't stay one little night longer. All this food'll go to waste.

(TODD enters from upstairs, carrying suitcases.)

BERTHA: Just take'em outside. Mr. Milrose is waiting. Brent! We have a plane to catch!

(BO extends his hand but TODD bypasses his hand and gives him a passionate hug. BO is motionless, dumbfounded. TODD exits onto porch with luggage and exits stage. BRENT enters from upstairs, carrying his fishing gear and sports bag.)

BERTHA: What in the world is all of this?

BRENT: What's it look like? A whale-honing device?
(Yells out the screen door.)
I call shotgun, Todd!

BERTHA: We're being driven to the airport in a pickup.

BRENT: A pickup? We're going to the airport in a pickup? That is so excellent! Todd ain't gittin' the back.
(Exits to porch and yells.)
Todd! I git the back! Y'all ride up front. I mean it, Todd. Ma's going to be crying anyways.
(Walks back into the kitchen and talks directly to PRECIOUS.)
Oh, sorry. I sure had a good time . . . Well, good for being at a funeral, well, two funerals.
(Pauses and then hugs PRECIOUS.)

(PRECIOUS is stunned with pleasant surprise.)

BRENT: Well, see ya.
(Runs onto porch with fishing gear and sports bag, and yells.)

I mean it, Todd!
(Runs off stage.)

BERTHA: Bye, Bo.

BO: Bye, little sister.

(They hug as PRECIOUS sits and prepares meal.)

BERTHA: Precious? I'm taking this one little pearl necklace. I don't want anything else. The house, the furniture, this is all yours.

PRECIOUS: That's predictable. Take the one most important thing that belonged to Mama.

(BERTHA removes necklace from her neck and places it beside PRECIOUS. She picks up her bag and walks to door.)

PRECIOUS: Wait, Bertha Sue.
(Retrieves a box wrapped in Christmas paper.)
I wuz savin' it fer Christmas, but maybe now's best. It's yer concert band second symphony.

(BERTHA hugs PRECIOUS tightly, looks around one more time, and exits to porch and off stage.)

PRECIOUS: *(Wipes eyes and walks to stove.)* There. All ready to be mixed in with ginger. Where's that Dwayne brother'a your'n?

BO: Buddy's.

PRECIOUS: I still say they ain't no good fer one another.

BO: Maybe not.

PRECIOUS: Why don't you like him?

BO: What?

PRECIOUS: You ain't nice to Dwayne Lee.

BO: I'm nice to him. We don't have much in common. Quit stirring up trouble where there isn't any.

PRECIOUS: Jest observin' truths.

BO: We don't have the same kind of friends.

PRECIOUS: Yer friends too good fer his?

BO: You said Dwayne and Buddy aren't good for one another. I didn't.

PRECIOUS: You said, "maybe."

BO: I said, "maybe," because if I said, "yes" or "no," I figured you'd argue with me.

PRECIOUS: Arguin' won't kill ya.

BO: I'm tired. It's been a heck of a week.

PRECIOUS: Mama says, "Laziness is no excuse fer hidin' yer heart behind yer brain."

BO: I'm not hiding.

PRECIOUS: Well then, yes or no, do you like Dwayne Lee?

BO: Uh . . . sometimes.

PRECIOUS: So, there are times you hate him.

BO: I didn't say, "hate."

PRECIOUS: If it's not true don't git flustrated.

BO: Okay, okay, okay. I hated it when Dwayne took Brent out back and showed him how to gun down that deer with a pistol.

PRECIOUS: You didn't mind eatin' no deer.

BO: I hated it at Mama's funeral how every time Sue Jean and the kids came around, Dwayne ran off to smoke, and I hated it even more when he came back smelling like liquor.

PRECIOUS: Yer welcome.

BO: What do you mean . . .
(Mocks her.)
"Yer welcome?"

PRECIOUS: A moment ago, you said, "maybe." Now yer ready to spit in Dwayne Lee's eye. Truth ain't purty, but it's truth. Yer welcome.

BO: I'm going upstairs.

PRECIOUS: Bo, sorry if I wuz hard on ya.

BO: You're not hard on me. You just annoy me a little.

PRECIOUS: A little?

BO: Uh uh. I'm not getting into this again.
(Exits upstairs.)

PRECIOUS: Don't fall off to sleep. I'll have dinner ready early!

DWAYNE: *(Enters from outside.)* Where is everybody?

PRECIOUS: Bo's upstairs restin'. Bertha Sue and the hunks left.

DWAYNE: *Left?*

PRECIOUS: Since when did you care if people come or went? Dinner'll be ready early.

DWAYNE: I ain't hungry.

PRECIOUS: Got ginger rolls and mashin' up Kennebec potatoes with lots'a peppers what you like.

(DWAYNE becomes silently anxious and paces.)

PRECIOUS: Why Dwayne Lee Reamy, you look like you seen a ghost. What's the matter?

DWAYNE: Nothin'.

PRECIOUS: I see everythin'.

DWAYNE: I can't believe how rude New-York-City drivers is.

PRECIOUS: You ain't never been to no New York City.

DWAYNE: I didn't say I had *went* to New York City. I jest said their drivers are rude. One had drove through Brantley Run yesterday, had *New York City* on his license plate. He blew his horn over and over at poor old, deaf Mr. Bloat on his tractor.

PRECIOUS: Dwayne Lee!

DWAYNE: What?

PRECIOUS: Why wuz you so outta kilter over a rude New York stranger?

DWAYNE: No reason.

(PRECIOUS stares him down.)

DWAYNE: I said no reason, Precious.

PRECIOUS: City folk bust through here lots and it don't phase you one iota.

DWAYNE: No reason means jest that, *no* reason.

PRECIOUS: What you gonna do with that four-hundred dollar?

DWAYNE: That's mine to do what I want.

PRECIOUS: Dwayne Lee!

DWAYNE: I need it fer gittin' a job.

PRECIOUS: A job? Oh, that's darlin'.

DWAYNE: Dreyton Hopper's papa's settin' up a construction company buildin' condominiums. He wants me and Dreyton to do electric wirin'.

PRECIOUS: You know about wirin'?

DWAYNE: Dreyton and Buddy learnt me nights, down at the Amoco.

PRECIOUS: Oh, Dwayne Lee! Does Bo know?
(Turns to yell upstairs.)

DWAYNE: No!

PRECIOUS: We'll tell him at dinner.

DWAYNE: I ain't eatin', Precious.

PRECIOUS: A big construction man? Papa and Mama would be so proud.

DWAYNE: Dreyton and his papa's haulin' out tonight. The condo project's down at the beach.

PRECIOUS: The beach?

DWAYNE: Virginia Beach.

PRECIOUS: That's clear 'cross Virginia. Too far to drive back and forth.

DWAYNE: That's why I need four-hundred dollar. First month's rent. After that, I'll make good money. Maybe Sue Jean and the kids'll see fit to join me.

PRECIOUS: Virginia Beach.

DWAYNE: I'll write you, Precious Grace. You wuz the onliest person who wrote me regular that long month in jail.

PRECIOUS: No!

DWAYNE: I gotta go.

PRECIOUS: *(Paces and talks faster, in a different tone, as if possessed.)* You'll go there and you'll drink!

DWAYNE: I stopped.

PRECIOUS: People who drink always say that. Take yer trashy friend Buddy with you. Grab a few loose women. Maybe Mr. Hopper can fix you up with a few.

DWAYNE: You sound like Mama in one'a her fits.

PRECIOUS: Fergit all the good Mama and Papa and me did slavin' over fixin' you meals and washin' yer clothes and bailin' you outta trouble time after time.

DWAYNE: Quit it, Precious.

PRECIOUS: Do you think Mama really wanted to have you, Dwayne Lee? She knowed you wuz bad blood before you got started.

(DWAYNE walks toward porch door.)

PRECIOUS: *(Blocks exit.)* The criminal element wuz jest waitin' to pop out when you got growed. You wuz born bad, you is bad, you'll always be bad—

DWAYNE: *(Screams.)* Nooo!
(Pulls back his fist as if he is going to slug PRECIOUS, but stops with his fist in the air.)

(PRECIOUS crouches with her hands up to protect herself.)

DWAYNE: *(Pauses to calm himself, and then slowly lowers his fist.)* Goodbye, Precious Grace.
(Exits outside and off stage.)

(PRECIOUS waits until she feels safe, and then slowly walks onto the porch and watches the distance.)

BO: *(Enters the kitchen, sets down his suitcase, and walks onto porch.)* What was all that commotion?

PRECIOUS: What?

BO: All that squalling.

PRECIOUS: Uh . . . Jest Dwayne Lee. He's went.

BO: Went?

PRECIOUS: Virginia Beach . . . Construction job.

BO: A construction job? For how long? Did he say when he'd be back?

PRECIOUS: Dwayne Lee's jest plain outright leavin' West Virginia.

BO: For good?

PRECIOUS: Sometimes I git this nightmare, Bo. Here's our little farm, settin' in the middle'a all these woods. Nice as it can be. But in the woods, far as inside yer head can see, there's bad voices sayin' ugly things and laughin' at us. At Uncle Dwezel, at Mama, at me and you. Hear'em, Bo? All 'round us. Watchin', listenin', waitin'.

BO: I don't have time for voices!

PRECIOUS: I can't stay alone, Bo. Somethin' awful's gonna happen.
(Sings gently.)
"Jesus, my Jesus is watchin'."

BO: Oh, this is great! Bertha and Dwayne both go running off and stick me with you. I should have seen it coming!

PRECIOUS: Bo? It won't be bad. Me and you. We can put the ole tire swing back up.

BO: Are you out of your mind? I have a life! What? I'm going to stay here and swing and water flowers on people's tombstones? Draw rainbows?
(Screams.)
Dwayne! For once in my life I really needed you!
(Exits into the kitchen and grabs his suitcase.)

Fine. Two can play this game.

PRECIOUS: *(Follows BO.)* You can't leave me, Bo!

BO: You won't let a nurse come here! You won't go to the hospital! Dwezel's dead! Eula's in Weston! What do I do? Huh? Drop you off at the emergency room and run?

PRECIOUS: Oh, Bo, I warned you. Didn't I? The cookies. The cookies, Bo. You took away Eula's cookies. You made Eula sick. You made Dwezel die. You took'em from me!
(She pounds BO's shoulders with her fists, causing him to drop his suitcase.)
It's yer fault, Bo! You broke Papa's and Mama's hearts!

BO: Calm down, Precious.

PRECIOUS: You hated Dwayne Lee and Bertha Sue so much they left me! Who do I have left, Bo? Who?

BO: Stop it, Precious!

PRECIOUS: *(Paces in a trance, hallucinating, mumbling.)* Why, maybe we could. Mama's butcher knife's in the oven drawer. It's still got little pieces'a yellow onion clingin' from that last time Mama held it.

BO: Stop it!

PRECIOUS: The turkey carvin' knife. We could use that one.

BO: Why, Precious Grace, what's tomorrow? I forget. A lightning day or a rainbow day?

PRECIOUS: Huh?

BO: Tomorrow? A lightning day or a rain—

PRECIOUS: Oh! A lightnin' day.

BO: Lightning day. So, you gotta water the flowers from nine-thirty—

PRECIOUS: Ten after nine 'til twenty-two after nine.

BO: *(Calmly helps PRECIOUS to sit in a chair.)* Ten after nine. Good. Lightning day. Precious, I need you to be strong for me, honey. Like Great Granny Blossom, when the Governor wanted to straighten out that curve by her porch.

PRECIOUS: Sit with a double-barrel on my lap and fire at bulldozers?

BO: Not exactly that strong.

PRECIOUS: I don't want no governor wrote down as my first major kill. People tend to fergit a person's life and focus on that one little incident.

BO: I suspect so.

PRECIOUS: Dwayne Lee's gonna win back that Sue Jean high-school beauty queen of his, ain't he?

BO: Sue Jean was never a high-school beauty queen. Dwayne lies about that.

PRECIOUS: In Dwayne Lee's eyes, Sue Jean won.

BO: I suppose so.

PRECIOUS: Sue Jean put a teddy bear next to her brother Owen's name at that Vietnam Memorial. That makes her good fer Dwayne. We could have such nice times here, Bo.

BO: I have a life waiting down the mountain. My boys, they ain't never heard about Crazy Harold, or rainbow days, or Eula's big freezer with the saw-mill chain. We ain't once in our lives sat around a table and talked. Really talked. Precious Grace, I ain't never letting go of you, or Mama, or our farm. 'Cause you're all in here.

PRECIOUS: *(Hallucinates and talks softly to self.)* No. I don't think he will. What? Okay. Maybe later.

BO: Precious?
(Looks around the kitchen, walks to record player, and plays a record. He returns to PRECIOUS and kneels beside her.)

(Sound of a slow rag, blues, or country song.)

BO: Miss Precious Grace Reamy, I presume? The Royal Knights of the American Revolution Ladies Auxiliary of Brantley Run extends us this exclusive inaugural invitation to attest to our tap and charm capabilities.

(BO extends his hand. PRECIOUS, puzzled, stares, not knowing what to do. Then she smiles, takes his hand, and giggles like an embarrassed schoolgirl. The two of them dance in an awkward waltz, PRECIOUS giggling. As the music completes, BO kisses her hand, turns her around in a dance movement, and escorts her to her seat. He quietly gathers his suitcase and belongings.)

PRECIOUS: *(Remains seated, motionless.)* Yer leavin'. Mama's gone. The magic's fadin'. What you wuz lookin' fer, Bo? Weren't out front somewhere. It wuz behind you.

BO: No chance you'd consider moving in with Sumter and me and the boys?

(PRECIOUS shakes her head.)

BO: Bertha and I talked. We'll call you every week.

PRECIOUS: Every week, then every month, then maybe Christmases.

BO: Mama and Eula's church circle promised to call on you.

PRECIOUS: They did? How sweet'a them. A church-circle-number-four visit. I could fix sassafras tea. Of course, Velma Moats requires Lipton.

(BO exits onto the porch, listens a moment, and then exits stage.)

PRECIOUS: What will I talk about? I gotta have a story. Mama always has a story.

(A single spotlight rises as the remainder of the stage dims. PRECIOUS walks into the spotlight.)

PRECIOUS: I'll tell them about the inaugural invitation, the time I had the loveliest dance. I'll say, "There wuz a wondrous August moon, the same moon that shined throughout Mama's dyin'. I was heartbroken as any dutiful daughter would be. In the shadow of my overwhelmin' grief, in walked this stranger, more handsome than anybody I ever seen. This stranger, this gentleman, walked right up, without so much as an introduction, bowed and kissed my hand, summoned me to dance."
(Pauses, looks at the ceiling, and screams.)
Not now . . . Later!
(Pause. Speaks softly.)
The woods is close. Hear them whispers, Bo? They's watchin'.

(Freezes for a moment, kneels, and clasps her hands in prayer position. She sings sweetly and softly, looking up at sky.)
"Jesus, my Jesus is watchin'. Watchin' over me . . . Jesus, my Jesus is watchin'. Watchin' . . . over . . ."
(Long pause.)

(BLACKOUT.)

About the Author

A native of the South, DC Fidler has combined a career in academic psychiatry and cultural psychiatry with a lifetime of playwriting, acting, directing, composing music, and teaching creative writing and the dramatic arts.

He studied theatre, writing, chemistry, medicine, and psychiatry at the University of North Carolina at Chapel Hill, where he served on the faculty. He later served on the faculty at West Virginia University, teaching cultural psychiatry, clinical psychiatry, and acting.

A licensed psychiatrist, DC Fidler has lived and worked with the Alutiiq tribe in Akhiok, Alaska, the Al Moqbali Bedouin tribe near Sohar, Oman, the Kalkadoon Aboriginal Tribe in the outback of Queensland, Australia, and the Te Tau Ihu Maori Tribes on the South Island of New Zealand.

He began his acting career in outdoor dramas, summer stock theatre, and local films and television at age ten. He has written scripts and composed music for over fifty medical educational videos at UNC-CH and WVU. He has written seventeen plays that have been produced in various community theatres and universities across North Carolina, Virginia, and West Virginia, as well as St. Louis, Sacramento, San Diego, Los Angeles, Boston, Chicago, and New York City.

He consulted and appeared in educational productions for HBO, ABC, and PBS and performed in numerous stage plays including: *Hope is the Thing with Feathers, Night of January 16th, Thieves' Carnival, Blood Wedding, Our Town, A Life in the Theatre,* and *Fool for Love.*

Presently, he is a scriptwriter, film director, and medical consultant for educational films using professional actors to demonstrate mental health issues. In addition, he is an active member of the Dramatists Guild of America and the Charlotte Writers' Club.

Fidler previously chaired the Video Committee for the American Psychiatric Association and served as President of the Association for Academic Psychiatry. In 2003, he was inducted as a Fellow of the Royal College of Physicians of Ireland. He serves on the Arts and Humanities Committee for the Group for the Advancement of Psychiatry where he is co-producing a video series on the History of Psychiatry, and using the arts to teach people about mental health.

He is author of the textbook, *Psychiatry for Actors: Using Psychiatric Principles to Build Characters,* and author of the novel, *Boogieban.*

Musicals by DC Fidler
- Pied Piper
- Healer Man
- Medicine Show

Plays by DC Fidler
- Voices in the Woods
- Guilt by Association (With RJ Casey)
- Three Diaries
- Master William Bowlinggreen and Company
- Shiraz
- The Anniversary of Miss Nanette Pringle
- School Children Hiding Under Desks
- Grams
- Camp Uni
- Boogieban (Two-Actor Version)
- Boogieban (Seven-Actor Version)
- Ahulaqs
- Elk and Wolf (With Travis Teffner)
- Santee Delta (With Travis Teffner)
- Celtic Crossing
- Stone Touchin'
- Daugherty Park Merry-Go-Round
- La Dynastie
- Gyges Solution

Short Plays by DC Fidler
- Persons
- Cruise
- Mobile to Where
- Oman Truce
- Second Amendment
- The Greek God Club
- Four X
- Microscopic Misconceptions
- Drone Guns
- Moon Bugs (WithTravis Teffner)

www.ingramcontent.com/pod-product-compliance
Lightning Source LLC
Chambersburg PA
CBHW051555280626
47162CB00022B/2316